THE LOST STORIES

THE LOST STORIES

L. MARIE WOOD

FALSTAFF
BOOKS
WWW.FALSTAFFBOOKS.COM

THE CLEANSING

THE FLAMES LICKED, danced, engulfed the wood eagerly like a hungry beast. She watched it flicker then build, climbing the walls like vines on the side of a house, undulating against the wall like lovers.

Wanting closure; wanting release. The orange glow, tinged with the faintest hint of blue, she knew, would give her peace.

BEYOND THE CHAIN

I used to want more.

I used to want to hear dogs barking, hear the laughter of children, get hit with the sprinkler every evening at dusk, and hope that baseballs didn't do any lasting damage. I wanted that, but what I got was a patch of grass hardly long enough for a grown man to lie down in heel —to —head, and trees so tall you could only see me in in the dead of winter, and then only if you squinted.

No dogs bark, no children play, not after they chained up the gate and took him away, not after what they found inside.

Gerald.

They never listened to him, not even when he swore he didn't know they were there, playing house in his shed, sitting around the table waiting for him to get home.

I knew they were there but I couldn't tell.

I wouldn't tell.

They couldn't make me. Nothing could.

I knew they were they there, but they shouldn't have been. They were trespassing. They weren't invited. They didn't belong.

He said he didn't know, but that was a lie. He had to have known. I secretly think he put them there. For me. I fancied that for years, imagining that he had brought them there for me to see, for me to play with. I thought of what his voice might sound like when he told me to do what I wanted with them, that they were mine to do with what I would. He would sound strong and confident, nothing like the whimpering imbecile they dragged away that day, wide-eyed and pointing at me. I fantasized that he lied to them to make them stay, and oh, what a good liar he turned out to be! Maybe he told them that everything he did was for them, and that they had nothing to worry about because he cared for them and always would. Maybe he told them that my soul spoke to him and that I loved them too and that I wanted them there as much as he did. Their stench still sits in the wallpaper they had lined the walls of the shed with, trying to make the place look like a proper home.

He lied to himself about them, about me, about it all. Even as he set fire to the weeping willow that had been my friend, the massive thing that had sheltered cardinals and bluebirds over its 250-year life—even as he tried to use to it to burn away everything he ever knew, he couldn't murder the truth, couldn't clean away the stain. Even as he sits in his cell, far away from me now, still he knows, he remembers, he feels.

The table is still set for dinner, modestly, for three servings instead of five. The pitcher upon the table, with the painted rooster on the side and the chipped spout, is empty now, but that can be easily remedied. All one need do is ask.

No one comes past the chain or ventures into the woods to peek anymore—that time has long gone. Now they pass by without a second glance at the overgrown driveway, the cracked asphalt barely visible beneath layer upon layer of dead leaves and weedy undergrowth. Someone left candy once, had thrown it past the chain and into the gaping maw that yawned behind it. I imagine a child being teased on Halloween when I think of it, their candy bucket snatched and ransacked by older kids. Perhaps they threw the candy inside and dared him to go after it. But it was only one piece of candy, hardly enough to dare with or risk repercussion for. No one ever came to get it. Had they come they might have seen me, might have said hello, might have dug into their eye sockets to pluck out the things that had betrayed them and shown them such a sight.

I would have shared the candy with them if they had.

SOMEBODY WAS CLAIRVOYANT

"WHAT DOES THIS ONE GO TO?"

She could feel the cool stream of sweat run from the base of her neck down her spine as his hand hovered over the yellow ethernet cable.

It should have been red.

Red meant stop, alarm, don't.

Yellow said come play with me in the sunshine.

It should have been red… like she said.

But they had all said no, no, let's keep it uniform, hide in plain sight, this is the way it should be.

And finally, the one that made her inner self laugh so hard her voice was nothing but a rasp at the end of it all, 'No one's ever gonna touch it anyway.'

Should she say something?

Saying something might make him want to touch it all the more. If she told him that this was the only cable in the place that mattered, the only one that could make everything go boom if he even jiggled it. That it would be back to card catalogs, back to typewriters, to chalkboards and rail travel, beyond jump drives to floppy disks and back before that.

Vinyl and talk radio. Kerosene lamps and carrier pigeons—he would set it all back, back, back, further than he could ever imagine if he just unplugged it. If he just…

No, she couldn't tell him that.

But if she said nothing…

"I said, what the hell does this one do?" he asked again, anger furrowing his brow and seeping into his voice. She forgot what she was up against while she daydreamed, forgot about the taser positioned under her jaw.

Fine.

Fuck it.

The cloud can disintegrate; data can be lost; DMs never answered, stories never be told. Vacation pics will be gone forever and contacts lost. Dick pics wiped from the face of the earth.

No more likes.

No more following.

No more friends.

It was her job to keep it all going, to protect the world… to protect the cable from water, heat, some asshole bumping into the rack and shaking loose a power cord. It was her job to make sure updates were applied and that the fans kept blowing. And there were others, others who were supposed to guard her, protect her from the outside, make sure her area wasn't breached, but they fell down on the job. Taking the water break she never had. Bullshitting about the game she'd never see or the weather she'd never feel because she was always in there, always there with the cable. They were screwing around while the cable was being threatened.

Fine.

Pull the damned thing.

"You got three seconds to tell me what the hell this goes to or —"

"Everywhere."

His eyes squinted in confusion.

"It goes everywhere. It does everything. It *is* everything."

He laughed incredulously, not knowing what else to do. His face twitched as he tried to put a response together, and she had to hold back a smile. She couldn't stop the words of a spiritual the old people used to hum from creeping into her head, almost sang them out loud. Maybe if she had it would have helped reset him. Maybe he would have just used the taser and this would all be over... for her, anyway.

"No shit?" he said and she couldn't help but think about how brilliant a response that actually was.

He looked at his hand still hovering just above the cord but trembling now.

She looked at him looking at his hand, thought of the war on the other side of the world actively transmitting locale coordinates over the dark web, and willed him to do it.

SHE

THE SMELL WAS LUXURIOUS.

It turned my stomach.

That from within the cabin I could still smell the eclectic perfume, a mix of fried chicken, wet pennies, and Eau De Toilette that only she could make sweet, made me weak-kneed. The scent, long cleared by earth and element, filled my nostrils as my mind first commands, then pleads, "You don't recognize, you don't recognize, you don't, you can't...."

But still, I do.

JUNK MAIL

HE SIGHED as he took out his keys and juggled the mail crammed in his hand. *Nothing but junk mail*, he thought. There never seemed to be anything important in the mail anymore. Unless...

Rick stopped in his tracks, one foot on the steps leading to the door of the brownstone, one still on the sidewalk. Maybe, just maybe...

He sifted through each circular announcing weekend deals, each request for help from local shelters, each bill, but there was nothing. Nasim had promised to send him a card with her new address on it. She had insisted on sending the note via snail mail—she liked the simple things. Sending a card instead of a text was right up her alley.

Just the thought of her choosing a card carefully, addressing the envelope in her steady hand, and dropping it in the mailbox made Rick smile. Then he felt that familiar tickle in his nose, the one that had been making an appearance every week or so since she announced she was moving to Boston. He never let her see, never let on that there was anything other than a friend missing a friend going on. There was so much more going on in his head though, especially since the dream job in Boston had become a reality. Happiness, frustration, sadness—all those emotions mingled inside him, bouncing off the walls, jostling as they vied for center stage. He felt angry with himself for never telling Nasim how he felt. They had been working together for years; their cubes were side by side. He saw her walk in and out every day, until she literally walked out of his life. They went to lunch together, jogged in the park on the weekends. She lived near his mother, which meant they bumped into each other at the supermarket, the coffee shop, the movies— everywhere. It was like they were supposed to be together. All he had to do was say something. But he never did. And then she left. Admiring someone from afar has its perks, but sometimes it just sucked.

Rick sorted through his keys, grabbing the battle-scarred gold one that fit his mother's door and thought about Nasim's smile. Not her mouth and the way it pinched at the corners to hint of dimples, as much as her eyes. They were so expressive; he couldn't bear to look at them for long. Recently her eyes held a sadness that was almost palpable. Could it be that she dreaded the thought of losing him as much as he did her?

Rick whipped his head toward Nasim's door. Maybe she would send him the picture they took in the office the day before she left. Rick wished it was of them alone, but Beth, the nosiest colleague in the office, jumped into the frame as if it was her rightful place. He'd have to deal with it—at least he got the chance to hold Nasim in his arms for a fleeting moment.

Rick almost dropped the keys when he saw the man looking in Nasim's window as his mother's door swung shut.

Maybe it was a potential new tenant coming to view the apartment. That would make sense since Nasim had just moved out, but that didn't make him feel any better. It was akin to a man marrying another woman as soon as his divorce is finalized. The ink on the paper wasn't even dry.

Rick watched as the man took a selfie with the apartment and then stepped into the vestibule to take a closer look. He choked back a sob and, instead, let out an audible sigh. Nasim was gone, had moved on and was starting the next chapter of her life somewhere else. Without him. If ever he needed a reality check, there it was.

Rick took the stairs to his mother's front door like a man with the weight of the world on his shoulders. He wanted to look over at Nasim's door again, but what was the use? He wouldn't see her smiling face looking back at him; her dancing eyes wouldn't sparkle with excitement because she wasn't there. She was never there. Her apartment was nearby —just a few blocks, really—but not across the hall where he could knock on the door with a pint of her favorite ice cream and an invitation to watch a late-night movie. Rick didn't even know if he was really seeing someone look through the window and into the apartment across the hall at all; that he could was implausible, if he was being honest. He'd have to look at just the right time to catch someone standing on the stairs outside the building, would have needed to time the door swings of both his mother's and the brownstone's front doors to allow him a second of unobstructed view of the street to notice someone looking into the unit that didn't belong to Nasim, that didn't belong to anyone he knew at all. It could all just be his imagination; the way things had been going since Nasim died, Rick couldn't tell anymore.

Rick squeezed his eyes shut, cutting fat tears in half to wet his eyelashes. The tickle in his nose was becoming unbearable, and his skin felt so hot, so very hot. And there was something else too, something Rick wasn't sure he truly understood... wasn't sure he really wanted to.

Rick breathed deeply, felt perspiration dot his brow, as he registered the smell clinging to the air in his mother's apartment.

RED NAIL POLISH

DAINTY. It's not a word I use often, but that's what her toes were. Small, delicate. They looked like they were handcrafted and never used, like the toes on a porcelain doll. Red nail polish on alabaster skin. Like a speck of blood on new fallen snow.

I smile when I think of it. I can be so poetic in moments like these, when it's quiet and dark. So witty in my mind, yet it never comes to my lips. My lips, pink and full of life, as usual are closed, my voice as silent as my captive audience's when people are near. And how could you blame me? What, with their sneering and snickering, their leering and salivating. The frozen smiles I set never sneer. To a poet, they listen. To an artist, they sit in awe. They are rapt. As they should be.

Red nail polish on unblemished skin. Dainty, like a girl rebelling for cotillion, a little spice beneath the frill. No one to see it except me. But to last for eternity.

HYPNOPOMPIA

THE NUMBERS SPUN—THEY spun!—right before my eyes, and I know I'm groggy, I know I'm having trouble waking up this morning, but I know that's not right. When I woke and looked at my alarm clock, bastard that it is, beeping incessantly like a truck backing up, high-pitched and monotone at the same time… when I woke up and looked at the time, it was steady. 6:33—I might have tried to ignore it for a few minutes and that's why it was 6:33 and not 6:30… sue me. It was overcast, but the sun was trying to peek through the blinds. I know that because I saw it. Everything was the way it usually was. Me not being able to haul my ass out of bed was normal too. Nothing to see here, folks, just your average Monday morning.

But I *did* get up. I didn't hit snooze this time. I trudged across the room like the walking dead, my eyes mere slits as I made my way to the bathroom, the commode, the sink, and then back into the bedroom. I sat down on the edge of the bed and put on the TV. A little news was what I needed, I thought, other voices in the room to coax me along. The distant thought I'd had last night about working out this morning was like a joke that some comedian had tried that fell flat. I had a moment to consider that I could dial my wake-up time back an hour if I was just going to let that fantasy go, felt the corners of my lips twitch in the beginnings of a smile at the thought before all was blank again. I fell asleep sitting up, remote in hand, and mouth wide open. I know that because I woke up that way too.

It couldn't have been long—*couldn't* have been. I would have fallen over or dropped the remote if it had been, right? Neither of those things had happened so I figured it had only been a few seconds, one of those moments where you doze off, are out of it so completely that you're disoriented when you wake up. I rolled onto my side, deciding to just give in, get another hour of sleep. I have a meeting in a few hours that I need to be sharp for and I was anything but that then. I laid down. Got into position to shut my eyes. That's when I saw it.

The guy on camera was talking about the weather—some storm system coming from the north that will cool temperatures and make it feel like Christmas in July. His back was turned, so I couldn't see his face, but what I did see made me sit bolt upright. His suit jacket was slit up the back and so was his shirt. There was raw, pink flesh peeking out beneath all of it. I could see a huge blister between his shoulder blades.

The temperatures showed on the map. At first it was just local, but then the map expanded to the United States, and then to the world.

"It's 90 °F in Calgary, but we're working on that. Parts of the US are hitting 175 °F and temps in Nigeria topped 325 °F last night. The Seine in Paris as well as the Canale Grande in Venice began to boil in the early morning hours. The Nile has boiled off completely, leaving lungfish and bolti to cook in the sun."

My mind couldn't process the words he was saying. I was distracted by the other data that was posted in the corners and running along the bottom of the screen:

Birds take flight in Florida only to burst into flames in the sky.

Woman fused to her car in Leeds.

Fissure opens in the ground to reveal lost ancient civilization beneath.

My mouth is open. I can hear myself panting.

The time on the screen, the one that I usually look at to confirm that I need to get up off my butt, get in the shower, and get going, was broken. The digital numbers were rolling, spinning, flying by. It was 6:45, then it was 7:22, then it was 3:14, then it was 5:58. It changed every second, and it was driving me crazy. Every time I tried to look at it, pin it down, see it clearly, it was something different.

And the world boiled.

"Do you want to go back to sleep? It might be best to stay in bed, sleep it off and wake up dead."

I looked at the weatherman, and he was looking back at me through eyes that had pushed out of their sockets to perch themselves outside of the skin, skin that was falling away in big, wet clumps. They moved independently of each other like bug antennae, and I couldn't stop looking at them.

They tipped toward me, almost like a man wearing a fedora might do his hat in greeting.

I smiled.

One of them winked at me.

I nodded.

BIDING TIME

THE CHAIR SPINS SLOWLY, teasing me, taunting me. I wait, bound by anticipation; raw and savage like the belt that cuts into my skin. Red streams into the wind like hair flowing in the breeze; spittle carried by the wind. Drops that stain the carpet fall in slow motion, reflecting what waits.

AFTERCARE

The polaroid was grainy, but that's how she liked it. Dim and from a bad angle, the picture captured everything she needed to see to spark the pleasant contraction in her lower half, the one that made her legs weak. She had hoped for this, wanted to feel the fresh excitement she was feeling at that moment, and she caressed the picture to express her thanks. Such a good boy. She would make sure the flowers she'd have delivered matched his suit.

MODEL HOME

THE LIGHT TURNED on in the darkness, a faint red glow indistinguishable in the unnatural greenish haze of night vision. Cabinets look creepy in the dark. So does the stillness of a sleeping house. Watching for too long can be terrifying —the feeling that something will show itself in the shadows is enough to drive someone mad.

Still, the camera came on for a reason...

Something floats before the lens. One would dismiss it as backscatter—indeed, most did that very thing—there is always dust in the air so the camera catching glimpses of it wouldn't surprise anyone except that shouldn't set off a motion-sensored security camera. If a camera can be calibrated to ignore a 25-pound cat, then surely it should be able to discount a speck of dust. If they watched long enough they would see the orb take a decided turn and cross in front of the camera once more before travelling deeper in the room and disappearing into the shadows. Another speck of dust? Not likely.

But they wouldn't look that long—most people didn't. Because that's not what they would be looking for if they turned on this feed. There were countless other feeds of this very room when the demons came out to play, their forms sometimes translucent when wandering specters entered lost or angry; sometimes solid flesh and blood as looters lifted and squatters broke, but none of those recordings would be important if anyone found out about this one.

If they noticed.

It's there, just a little bit of heel, but still there, in view if you looked hard enough. But would they? Was anyone ever really looking anyway? It's late—past 3:30 a.m. Who would be looking at this hour anyway?

They wouldn't see in time, wouldn't be able to save him, this man whose heel is the only thing in the recording. A dark, solid colored sock—Black? Blue?—still covered the toes, but the heel was bare... brown skin against a backdrop of shadows in a darkened house in the middle of the night. Infrared will pick up something, make the heel more visible if nothing else, but what good would that do? From such a distance and without the benefit of the toes it won't look like much of anything—it could be a Styrofoam cup just as easily as the only thing visible of a dying man. And no one would think a Styrofoam cup suspicious, not with as many people that come in and out of this place every day. People were always in and out, picking up things, stealing things, chatting up the agent but never intending to buy. Sometimes the realtor invited her boyfriend over to have sex. Sometimes she hooked up with one of those people who had entered the house that day wandering, wandering, just like those wayward spirits. But the camera was never on then, so nobody ever knew. But it's on now—does it make a difference?

They brought him here to dump him, did away with the alarm before any notification could be sent, but not the camera sitting inconspicuously on the hutch, the one that had the broadest arc of the room. Different system—one of the really good ideas that the team designing the newer model homes came up with, because petty thieves wouldn't think outside of the box about a thing like that. As far as they were concerned, the place was empty at night which made it prime pickings. Snip, snip on the wires, use some computer geekery to screw up the Wi-Fi and you're in.

But these weren't thieves.

They brought him there to dump him, but he wasn't dead yet. They carried him in, left him there on the floor, and walked out, never realizing that he would squirm a little before he died, moving just enough to bring his heel into view, never realizing that he would add his low moans to the sounds of the house settling.

If the design team had thought about manning the camera, periodically watching live, they would have seen it. But they never would have saved him.

An orb shot out of the room followed by another, heading right for the camera, on the heels of the first. They were racing each other, like children in a park, flying so quickly they almost looked like a streak. An old friend coming to pick him up, showing him it was all right and now they would be together forever? Perhaps. Backscatter to those who might look after the body was found, just dust floating in the air, if they saw it at all.

IMPURE

HE SAT in the shadows watching her as she moved, savoring the way the light caught the red in her hair, the way her chin dipped slightly to the left as she thought. He was tempted—that went without saying. But it went beyond the innate desire to satisfy the burning in his lap. Indeed, his hand resting there, absently stroking, was far removed from his thoughts. Instead he spoke to her, told her exactly what he wanted to do to her. He caressed the words, leaving them silky and smooth. He reached for her and felt her rise to meet his waiting hand.

The silence served to mask his passion, and he was happy for it.

No distractions. Nothing but him.

From the recesses of her mind she felt him pressing, his heat permeating her mind, exploring her with an eagerness that made her moan. She looked around the room to find herself alone, as she knew she was... as she wished she wasn't.

LEVEL-UP

THE ROOM WAS DARK, but not completely; the waning light seemed to glow on the other side of the blinds. When they started the movie it was still light outside, but as the hours went on and the movie started getting good, no one had gotten up to close the blinds all the way.

The TV screen was dark—only the outline of a woman, her hair sweated out into long, stringy strands that stuck to her face, the only thing they could see. Her breath pushed the strands in the front away from her face every time she exhaled.

In.

Out.

In.

Out.

Faster with every second.

She was going to make herself pass out soon, hyperventilate or something. It was too much too soon.

"Overacting," Gabe said, and Wally nodded in agreement. It was ridiculous. Indie films either had really amazing acting or such shitty performances that it seemed like the actors were somebody's cousin or sister. This one was the latter, down to the smeared convenience store mascara that had managed to run all the way down her cheeks and dip under her chin before diluting.

She fumbled and found her phone, told the audience she was having trouble finding the flashlight function on it by hemming and hawing and 'Oh no!'-ing and 'Damnit!'-ing. When she finally found it, she had the nerve to say,

'Ok, found it!' before turning it on, as if they wouldn't have known she had when she illuminated the room. Gabe and Wally expected there to be something behind her, something grotesque and freakish, but only as far as a doctored Halloween mask could go. They hadn't seen the thing chasing her yet—the whole thing had been very *Cloverfield*-esque so far—but the free soundtrack they'd downloaded off the internet was building, crescendoing in a way that was supposed to make viewers' backs arch, make them sit up taller in their seats. They'd oblige—the movie was working hard enough for it, so why not?

But there was nothing.

Good on them.

Wally let out the breath he hadn't realized he was holding, and Gabe chuckled, probably because he had done the same thing too. As corny as the movies they always ended up watching were, he loved them—the jump scares, the stupid decisions, the predictability. He loved all of that shit.

The girl onscreen inched forward, moving painstakingly slow.

All of a sudden there was no soundtrack anymore, and Wally couldn't put his finger on when it had stopped.

Ingenious.

It was quiet.

So very quiet.

And then three things happened all at the same time, though Wally would never admit one of them out loud.

The lights went out on the screen right when his brother came into the room asking what they were watching. And Wally, well, he almost jumped out of his skin.

"Never heard of it before," Eddie had said when Gabe told him the name of the movie. "Sounds cool! Can I watch?"

"No!" they'd yelled in unison. Wally knew he had shouted because Eddie had scared the hell out of him. He wondered if he had done the same to Gabe.

"Come on!" Eddie whined like clockwork. It was always the same.

'Can I watch?'

'No!'

'Why?'

'Because.'

'Because why?'

'Because I said, now go before I tell mom.'

Wally didn't really feel like going through it again, but there they were.

"Because—" Wally started but Eddie stopped him.

"Because you said," he said, defeated.

"Why'd you even ask, then? You could have just kept on walking instead of messing up the movie."

"Yeah," Gabe said, turning back to the TV where the woman was now backing up wide-eyed and comically terrified. It would take her at least 30 seconds to get on her mark so that the guy in the gorilla suit could jump out and scare her. She was probably going over and over how she'd execute her big horror movie scream in her head as they watched.

"You scared the shit out of Gabe," Wally said, fighting to keep a serious look on his face as he looked over at his friend. He failed.

"Me? You're the one who almost got air. *You* surprised me more than Eddie did."

"Oh, so you admit that you were surprised, which is just code for scared?"

They laughed.

The girl screamed on cue.

Gabe and Wally turned to watch.

So did Eddie.

It took Wally and Gabe longer than it should have to realize that Eddie was watching the movie, committing *Mutant Antennae* to memory as much as he could. All three of their heads were turned toward the screen, lured in by the feelers that left a viscous residue on the girl's skin after swiping at it, stretching across it, poking at it. And she screamed and screamed and swung her head around, more hair sticking to her face with every turn.

But then Gabe saw Eddie, mouth open, jaw slacked, eyes wide. He nudged Wally. Wally looked and had time to wonder how much trouble he would be in when Eddie woke up with nightmares for the next few weeks.

"Yo!" Wally yelled and stood up, blocking the TV from view. Eddie's eyes cleared, his vision no longer of the carnage onscreen but of his brother who didn't look happy at all. He wanted to bite it back, but he couldn't, the response more knee-jerk than anything.

"Hey! Get out of the way!" Eddie whined.

Always whining.

"Get out of here, man. You've seen enough already."

Wally walked around the sofa to where his brother stood trying to make his body heavy, hard to move. Gabe had sprung into action and paused the movie already so no more damage could be done, and Eddie hated him for it.

"I'll tell mom you let me watch," Eddie tried, but immediately wished he hadn't. He looked up to his brother too much to get him in trouble over something like that, and Wally knew it.

"You do that and I'll tell her what really happened," Wally said in response, playing along, and Eddie knew they were good. "Just go to your room—do some homework or something. It's almost over anyway."

Eddie left reluctantly, and Wally waited for him to go, listened for the door to the basement to open and close again signaling he was really gone. He didn't know how he missed it the first time, didn't understand how he missed the sound of Eddie's footsteps coming down the stairs, but he had. But not this time. Wally even leaned over to see if the kid had tried to trick him, had only opened and closed the door without going through it. He hadn't. Eddie was gone.

"It's like some kind of bug or something," Gabe said when Wally came back and sat down. The image on screen was that of the girl, her mouth open in a scream, looking behind her at the antennae reaching for her again.

"Duh," Wally said and pointed to the movie title displayed on the paused scream. "I kinda figured it would be."

Gabe laughed good-naturedly and continued, "No, I mean it's like some kind of ant. I would have thought it would be like a fly or something like that."

"What, like Mothra or some shit?"

"Something like that, yeah. Something that could lift people off the ground and drop them. Who's gonna be afraid of an ant?"

"Ants are beasts, though," Wally said, reaching for the bag of chips on the table between them. "Battle strategies have been formed around ant behavior."

"Yeah, but other bugs eat ants. Even butterflies eat ants, bro."

Wally laughed—there was no comeback that made more sense.

"They could have made it be a spider or something scary looking," Gabe continued, thinking.

Wally shook his head no.

"Been done way too many times. It's like with any horror movie set in Egypt—you know there's gonna be a mummy. Or if you see an Asian girl with her hair covering her face, you know it's one of those ghosts like the girl from *The Ring*. Enough with that shit."

"I mean, they try to change it up," Gabe said, settling into the conversation. "Zombies run now."

"True, but they aren't any stronger than they were before. You may not be able to outrun them now but you might be able to beat them. They're weak. The weakest link," Wally laughed, proud of the connection he made.

"What the hell are you talking about 'the weakest link'? Zombies are tough as hell. Remember the first episode of *The Walking Dead*? That woman was cut in half on the ground still trying to get at Rick."

"Yeah, and all anybody would have to do is side-step her. You don't even need to waste a bullet." They laughed because it was true, both of them remembering that scene in the show and nodding in agreement. "If a human can beat it, anything can."

"A mummy can't beat a zombie," Gabe said.

"A mummy *is* a zombie," Wally retorted. "And so is Frankenstein, so let's take them both out of the equation."

"Some people say Frankenstein isn't a zombie 'cuz he's a bunch of body parts put together. The new thing was never alive like that before."

"Yeah, and some people would go back and forth with us about how Frankenstein isn't the monster at all—that he was the doctor—even though they know damn well which one we're talking about right now."

"True. But he could be a golem."

Wally looked Gabe like he had grown two heads and kept going.

"Ok, so how about this. A werewolf can beat a zombie for sure because its gonna tear it up, rip its body to shreds."

Nodding, Gabe said, "Yeah a zombie wouldn't have a chance against a werewolf. And a vampire would completely kick a zombie's ass."

"Absolutely. A zombie wouldn't be able to catch it if it tried. A vamp could shapeshift into mist or a bat or whatever. Plus it could look into its eyes and Bella Lugosi it, tell it to go away."

"If its eyes weren't already rotted out," Gabe corrected. "But yeah, even if a zombie could catch a vampire, it couldn't do anything with it. Its body would be too hard to destroy."

Wally nodded and then thought of something.

"Come to think of it, a werewolf wouldn't be able to kill a vampire either. It would break its teeth on it.

Gabe nodded slowly.

"A ghost," Gabe started, rifling through his memory banks to find the information he wanted. "Dude... a ghost may be the baddest of them all."

"How do you figure?" Wally asked, his mind filling with images of long black hair and pale faces.

"Because it chooses how it manifests, right? So if it stays all see-through and shit, nothing can get a hand on it. You'd have to go destroy the body or get someone one to clear the house and get it out, exorcise someone, what have you. By the time that happens, the ghost could have already fucked shit up and taken off. A ghost wouldn't even waste time trying to beat a zombie—it wouldn't have to. It could just stay invisible. And then what? The zombie wouldn't even see what was dismembering it, picking up poles and shoving them through its skull. Boom. Over. Next."

A smile crept onto Gabe's face that spoke of a new understanding of everything important. "It's the Ultimo."

Wally smiled too now, the name bouncing around in his head and coming out good. When he spoke it, his voice was nothing short of reverent.

"Ultimo."

Eddie shook his head from his perch on the stairs as he listened to them talk about things they did not understand. They didn't understand who Ultimo was, what power he wielded. The fact that they spoke his name so randomly upset him, but he had to remember that they were ignorant. Yes, there was an Ultimo, but it wasn't any of those characters his brother and friend had been talking about. No. Ultimo was so much more than that.

Fast.

Strong.

Skin like armor.

Eyes like lasers.

Respawn capabilities.

He could shapeshift into any animal and any person—could speak whatever language the people around him were familiar with… in fact, they heard their language in their ears when he spoke, regardless of how many people were in the room.

He was fearless.

Ageless.

Didn't require oxygen to breathe nor food to eat. He definitely did not drink blood, could walk in the daylight if he wanted to and stay up all night if that was the plan. He was impervious to zombies and werewolves—his being was like metal to them, so they never tried to attack. He was deaf to sirens and poison to insects. He showed himself as Slender Man, Candyman, Freddy Kruger, Kayako, The Babadook to keep people at bay. Because if they knew about him—about who he really was—he would have to correct the situation.

He could use all weapons but he didn't need them—he *was* the weapon.

Nobody controlled him and all feared him.

He was Ultimo.

And Eddie knew just where to find him.

I HAVE NOTHING TO WEAR

HOW DOES THIS GO?

What do you wear to something like this?

Choker, accentuating the neck? V-neck to show more skin? Tight dress, short dress, loose dress, long dress, no dress, maybe pants instead?

Do you wear a jacket, a vest, ruffles, lace?

My hand lands on a crushed velvet top with buttons and strappy things, none of which I remember. When did I buy this?

Sequins?

No.

Burnout? That paper-thin material that always seems like it will rip and show off the things it barely concealed in the first place?

Maybe that. Yes, maybe so.

Do we dance or is this one of those drinking and smoking parties? I wouldn't mind feeling a body next to mine, pressed up close, hot breath on my neck—

Yeah, I'd better make sure my neck is out instead of in so I can feel all the sensations I am supposed to feel.

So…

Flower or stripes? Polka dots? Midriff shirt and leather shorts?

Damn, it's been a long time since I went out.

But he called and he's hungry and I want.

Black lace with a matching bra beneath and those same leather shorts I was thinking about before because he likes the way I look and them.

Maybe the others will too.

Maybe she'll tell me so and lick her lips, anticipating what my neck will taste like, wishing she was at the fount, lapping sucking, coaxing out more with every heartbeat.

Maybe he would grab her, spirit her away to sink his teeth in the other side, the unblemished side, claiming it for his own.

Lace scoop with the prettiest scalloped neckline for my coven divine.

THE SCIENCE OF IT

THE POT on the stove wobbles because it's too big for the burner, the middle warping and rising up into an arc as the heat turns the core red hot.

The pot on the stove wobbles because there's moisture beneath the metal and it's changing into something new, into something different, before it dissipates, dissolves, disappears.

The pot on the stove wobbles because he isn't quite dead yet, the nerves causing eyes to flutter and cheeks to rise in a smile, a grimace as flesh too fresh to know it's dead singes against the side.

GLASSES

I WENT BACK FOR THEM.

I went back because I knew he dropped them and someone would see.

I saw them fly off his face and land in the mulch, one frame obliterated by the blast and the other cracked and splintered—ruined beyond repair. They wouldn't need to be repaired, though; his blood smeared on the rim, on the lens, all over his face and hair, doubling back to mingle with what pooled in the gash at the top of his head told me so.

I went back for them.

I went back for them because I knew he'd want me to. I knew he'd like to have them with him wherever his body ended up, likely at the bottom of the quarry past the old farm because it was abandoned and the water was murky, filled with old shit that had sunk there decades ago—not even the sex-crazed idiots over at the high school used that spot for a romp because it was... there was just something off about it.

He'd like that.

If he had to die, he'd like to make a difference, and so I

would put his body there. There he could be part of the lore, be one of the ghosts that haunted that old, shut down place.

Plus, nobody would think to look there because nobody would have the guts to.

I went back for them, and they were there, right where he left them, right where they landed when they fell off after his eye was ruined and his face collapsed, little bones poking through the skin, piercing, cutting, flaying.

Except they were different.

They were bloodless.

The temples—arms, I called them, but he knew what the real word was... of course he did—were folded as though he had taken them off on purpose and laid them down.

But he hadn't.

He hadn't had the chance to do anything, least of all set his glasses up nice.

I went to pick them up but didn't because somebody must have done this and the realization washed over me like a cold breeze. Ok, an animal could have come and licked the blood clean, got a little appetizer before its main course. That made sense. But no animal could fold those arms—temples, shit— that way. Not a single one.

I went back for the glasses alone, in the dark. Nobody knew I was coming because if they did, they would know I had a body in my trunk and maybe even how that body got there.

I was alone out there and now it seemed darker than it was before, darker when I let loose the shot that lit up the sky and blew up his head, darker than I've ever seen it before.

Was he still there... watching me?

Why did we always think it was a 'he', anyway? It could be a 'she' just as easily because there's some sick bitches out there too—just as sick as some of the dudes I know. It's ridiculous to just think men—

What the fuck? I hate when I got off on a tangent, thinking about something stupid instead of paying attention to the shit happening in front of me. Because somebody fucked with his glasses and they could be—

I went back for them because I knew he'd want them but maybe I should have let them go. The leaves crunching under some bastard's foot told me so.

SAY CHEESE

BLOOD on the viewfinder draws fangs from smiles and opens wounds that bake in the noonday sun.

SUNDAY MORNING

1

HE STOOD ON THE STEPS, listening to the choir lift their voices, a last-minute practice before the morning's service. He wished he could plug his ears, blot out the sound with his screams, something. He didn't want to hear them thanking God for their lot in life, for the streets that stank like piss and vomit, for the bread and milk the government let them have for free. He didn't want to open those heavy doors and feel the oppressive heat greet him. It was cooler outside. He didn't want to smell the foyer, its odd mixture of incense, sweat, and sulfur ever present. He couldn't bring himself to bow his head in supplication again. He didn't feel anything when he did anyway—just the hot, sticky sweat that coated his neck cooling in the air that had been whipped up by the dirty fan propped in the window.

But he had to.

Just as sure as he knew his own name, he knew he had to enter that place, hear those sounds, and smell those smells again. The thick, glossy tenement paint that caked the walls had his name etched in it. The hymns that the choir wailed incessantly spoke to him this time... every time. At least that's what it felt like. He was afraid of what would happen if he didn't respond to their deafening call.

He opened the doors to the church—big hulking things made of dark wood with antique gold trim—and slipped inside. He didn't want to make a sound, didn't want to draw attention to himself. He just wanted to do what he had to do and leave. He might never come back if he could get away clean.

"Where you been, Caleb? You know he been looking for you."

The sound of the old woman's voice startled him. She was there, sitting on her perch like she always was, her Sunday outfit covered by a thick black shroud with her head bowed as if in prayer. A stack of fans advertising Bedman's Funerary Services sat on her lap, waiting to be handed to the parishioners that would fill the sanctuary soon. Everything was the same as it always was inside the church where he had begged for forgiveness all those years ago, his knees bruised and bleeding. This Sunday morning was the same as every Sunday morning, yet the scene frightened Caleb to the core.

The old woman didn't look up when she spoke.

He passed by her without responding. There was nothing to say anyway.

He had been gone for too long.

2

THE COGNAC CAP toe lace ups had been polished to a perfect shine. The gray slacks he wore touched the tops of the shoes, fitting the pastor the way only tailor-made clothing could. His robe, pressed crisply, fell mid-shin. He was smoothing it when Caleb entered the room. As the pastor took off the onyx ring that sat majestically on his right pinky, Caleb spoke.

"Hello, Pastor."

"There you are," the pastor said in a rich baritone. There wasn't happiness in his voice, but not anger either—frustration, perhaps. Caleb had been gone for longer than anticipated. He had almost caused a delay in the festivities.

Caleb closed the door behind him, knowing that was what was expected of him. He tried to remain quiet and still, wanting to say nothing under his gaze, but his will was weak. It would take a much longer absence for Caleb to escape the pastor's control.

The pastor waited in silence; his will was far stronger than Caleb's could ever hope to be. An explanation was expected, and Caleb knew he had better give one or suffer the consequences.

"They've taken to the streets again," Caleb started, trying to buy time. He glanced out of the window and saw the first of the congregation making their way to the weathered doors of the church. Sister Clara and her niece Magnolia were early, and Caleb had an idea why. He didn't have much time.

"St. Augustine Baptist is out there with their pastor sitting on a throne hoisted up on their shoulders," Caleb continued, trying to act normal even as he spied more people heading to the church doors, snatching glances at the upstairs window as they did. Brother Charles made eye contact with Caleb and nodded. Caleb wasn't sure if he nodded in kind or not. "They're carrying him around and singing hymns up and down 5th."

"Is that so?" The pastor groomed his mustache in the mirror, pulling his lips into a frown as the little comb tugged at the coarse hair.

"People are paying attention." Caleb didn't know why he said it. He shouldn't have, if he wanted to get out of there unscathed. But it was out, and Pastor heard it. He turned around with eyes ablaze.

"They can look all they want, can't they? Stick their heads out the window and watch the parade go by. But we know what we have here. We know where the true message of salvation lies, don't we Caleb?"

Caleb could already feel the pastor's cold, clammy hand on his arm, and he shivered. He didn't think he could bear the man touching him, not another time, but he had to. If he wanted to make it out of that room, he had to.

The pastor's hand stopped in mid-air, his eyes trained on Caleb's face. He studied the younger man, letting his gaze course over Caleb's nervous, darting eyes and sallow skin animated by trembling muscles. After what seemed like five minutes, he dropped his hand, busying it with something else; dusting his robe, slicking his hair back—Caleb didn't know. What the pastor did with his hands after the fact didn't matter. The smile that played at the corners of the pastor's mouth did.

Caleb began to pant—open-mouthed and shamefully.

The pastor walked away from Caleb and toward a desk that took up most of the small room. In an amused voice that belied a secret Caleb would never know, he asked, "Why you been gone so long, boy?"

Caleb's mouth felt dry. He couldn't peel his tongue from the roof of it.

"I—I had to go uptown to get what you needed."

"Is that so?" the pastor asked, his back turned to Caleb now as he fingered the hymnal on his desk. "And did you get what I need? Because you know I need it for today—right now, in fact."

"I didn't, Pastor. See, that's the thing," Caleb started. He knew the fidgeting and fast-talking he had started up was going to make everything worse, but he couldn't stop himself. "They didn't want to give it to me," he continued. "They told me you would have to get it yourself this time, or they can't help us no more."

Caleb inched toward the door as he spoke, focusing on it, thinking he might have to make a break for it before long. The pastor did not like to be disappointed.

"Didn't give it to you, you say?"

The pastor's voice seemed like it was coming from all around him. Caleb turned his head toward the desk where he had been standing but didn't see him there. He turned left and right but did not see him in either place. An involuntary gasp escaped his lips as the realization that the pastor was nowhere to be seen hit home. He decided that if he ever had a chance of getting away, it was then. Right then.

Caleb turned to the door and grabbed the handle. It was hot to the touch. Hissing in pain, he threw the door open and ran down the hall, barreling past the old woman so quickly he didn't notice that she was slumped over on her side at an unnatural angle, the fans that sat in her lap pooling around her feet like water.

Caleb ripped open the church doors, pulling them with such strength he almost ripped them off their hinges. He was almost out. He could feel the fresh air on his face, could smell the fragrance of the city: hot dogs, motor oil, and cigarettes all rolled up into one. He could be free if he could just take one more step.

Caleb put one foot onto the church steps that led to the door in triumph and cast a glance over his shoulder. The pastor stood before the amassing congregation, smiling with teeth that were unnaturally white. He carried on conversations and shook hands, all the while his eyes focused on Caleb.

His smile turned Caleb's blood cold.

CALEB LEFT the church feeling numb. He stumbled down the stairs, bumping into people on their way up, grabbing onto them for balance.

"What's the matter with you, boy?"

"You're going the wrong way!"

People pulled at him from all directions, trying to redirect his steps.

"No," Caleb exclaimed weakly, fighting to move away from the church steps and out into the world, the free world, where no one knew his name.

Where no one wanted anything from him.

"You know what I need, Caleb."

The pastor's voiced sounded inside his head. Caleb slapped his hands over his ears and howled in the morning light. He felt his legs give way, the concrete biting into the scars on his knees, splitting open skin that had long since healed from the last time he acquiesced under the weight of the pastor's gaze. His chest heaved with exertion as he screamed over and over and over again.

When his breath gave out and he lay gasping on the

ground, he lifted his head and looked toward the church doors knowing he had to see, but afraid of what he might find. The splintered wood seemed to jut out at him like daggers. The antique gold that had once outlined a lattice-work of symbols adorning the door had melted into a ruddy stream, donning an ancient patina the color of dried blood.

The congregation stared at him in expectation.

DARKNESS AND LIGHT

IT WAS DARK, but I could see as if the sun were shining, as if the blackness that engulfed the night was nothing more than shade from a tree. It writhed there, its body moving in waves, the vibration unconcealed by its paper-thin skin. It could smell me. I knew that. It could taste the salty-sweet scent of my fear on the air in a way that a true sommelier understands the composition of fine wine. But its anticipation had a scent also; one so enticing it woke me from my sleep. It salivates there in the woods, waiting for me to turn away, to unwittingly expose my neck to its teeth. I knew that too and would happily oblige, for a meal is a meal. And as the door locks behind me and the pulsating in my hands begins to ache, I wait to be sated as well.

THE CONVERSATION

"I DON'T WANT TO GO."

"What? Come on… you have to."

"Maybe I—"

"Maybe nothing. You already said you would—you can't just—"

"I said that years ago. I was a kid. He shouldn't have taken it so seriously. How could I say I would—"

"Wouldn't you?"

"Wouldn't I what?"

"Wouldn't you take it seriously? If you were getting everything you ever wanted, wouldn't you take it seriously?"

"How can he hold me to that, though? I was too young. It's—it's not…"

"Fair? Stop being ridiculous. There's no —"

"What are you talking about 'ridiculous'? How is it ridiculous? This is bullshit! I was too young to agree to something like that! No one in their right mind would hold me to —."

"—stupid."

"What? Why…"

"Are you kidding me right now?"

"I'm fucking serious. I'm not go —"

"And that's why I said you're stupid. He'll never go for it."

"Wha —"

"I mean, you know that, right? You can whine about how unfair it is and how you were too young, wah wah, but it's not gonna matter."

"You don't know —"

" —not now. Not ever, probably. It's gonna happen."

"I —I can't... I can't do it. I just can't."

"You will. You will and then you'll wish you'd never opened your mouth, never looked his way... never called him in the first place."

"No... I —I can't —"

"Hun, you don't have a choice."

ANOTHER DAY

IT RAINED the day I took them, trapped them, kept them inside—clear, where I can see. I took them all, let them settle, mingle, comfort each other as they rippled, moved, fought against the confines, their pretty little place, until they stilled.

No, not all of them.

Some I sampled. I couldn't make myself wait, not knowing when the day would come when I could visit with them again. So, I tried them—I tasted them. And I loved them.

I looked at them, those from that first day, that rainy day under a sky that seemed to hate me for what I was doing, sought to stop me by growling and clapping its hands. I looked at them every time I added another, even if I never looked at the other so often, never so intensely. I looked at them, and they saw me too. They called my name and it made me smile. Sometime the rain came again when I was looking at them, but it was less effectual each time, pouting instead of raging, punished, put in its place.

It rained today, and I took them out in spite of it, because of it. And tasted again. Tasted nearly each of them, leaving myself with almost none. Because it is another day, and I've saved for this... just like you told me to.

OUT OF TIME

RUNNING.

Blind, aimless movement, like a wave crashing onto the shore, rolling over and flattening the sand, removing all distinguishing marks: the hearts carved by fallen branches, the initials inside.

K. T.

+

L. M.

4 eva

Or at least until the tide came in and wiped it all away.

Wiped away.

Obliterated.

Razed.

Like Gomorrah and the Ark.

Starting over.

Starting again.

Hands pushed and grabbed. Legs pedaled, propelling men, women, and children toward the back of the store. The sweater she had been looking at seemed to disappear into thin air as if part of a magic trick—now you see it, now you don't—the garden variety activity provided for the very old and the very young at resorts when the parents go off to play. It had been ripped out of her hands by someone running by, face a blur. The tag came off in her hand, one of its corners puncturing her skin to draw blood. She thought to put the wound to her mouth and lick at it in that vampiric way that people did when they saw their own blood in the open air, selfishly recalling it into their own bodies before anyone else could partake. She thought to do so, to taste the metallic notes, but as the next person to barrel through the racked space nearly bowled her over, taking that route instead of the tiled path that was mobbed with runners from the café at the front of the store, the customer service section, and the bathrooms, she thought better of it. If her hand was in her mouth and she took another hit she might knock her own teeth out. She might bite so deeply into her flesh that the soft lapping of her tongue wouldn't be enough to assuage the pain.

Running.

Everyone was running. Yet their feet made no sound.

Because of the siren.

The siren started up, crescendoing to its highest point within seconds, its tone even and persistent. It sounded like an old-time ambulance, deep and full, not shrill even though the hair on her arms and the back of her neck stood up, responding to it the same way it did to high-pitched noises. She had always thought the gooseflesh came because of the shrieking nature of it all: babies crying, nails scratching on a chalkboard, the undertone of a fire alarm—that shrill beeping that seems to ring in the room even after the alarm has been turned off: all of it was enough to set her teeth on edge.

But that wasn't it.

That wasn't all.

The siren was going off.

The one that most people living there had never heard before, including her.

The siren that meant it was over.

Everything they knew was unequivocally, irreconcilably over.

Because They were there.

She watched an old man fall to his knees a few rows over from her. He had been in the toddler clothing section, perhaps shopping for his grandson, the one he would never see again because he would never get out of that store. She saw him drop to his knees because the racks that had separated his body from view just seconds before had been pushed aside, toppled, fallen upon. And there were bodies. Arms and limbs tangled, twisted, bent under the weight of their own bodies. Still. She felt her mouth open, felt her jaw unhinge as her eyes fell upon some of the bodies stacked on top of each other: big, small, tiny.

Tiny.

And there was blood.

THEY were there.

She tried to take a step, to run with the rest of them, to succumb to the understanding, the stark reality the older man had already allowed, to *move*, but she could do nothing, nothing, nothing at all as she thought of her parents probably trying to get into the basement, to get into the tub, to hole up like it was a tornado. She could do nothing as she thought of her dogs running around her house, ears flattened to their heads to block out the sound, whimpers escaping their throats—could imagine them bouncing nervously as they peered through the sliding glass door into their familiar yard, though that space likely didn't look so familiar anymore. She thought of her colleagues running into the storage closet like she would have if she hadn't gone out to lunch, pressing their bodies into a space filled with things that could kill them if turned into projectiles, but having nowhere else to go. And it wouldn't matter. Because this wasn't a hurricane; this wasn't a tornado, or a tsunami, or dust storm, or any other kind of storm. It was Them.

It was THEM.

And it was time.

She stood there, looking out of the store window, marveling at how much she could see now that there were no racks or display stands in the way. She could see the whole parking lot, the kaleidoscope of colors that the cars made. She could see the neon signs atop the storefront doors, noticed their names as they blinked out one by one, a backwards stadium wave, a wink, a caps off goodbye as the ground opened and then the clouds parted, asphalt, concrete, wind, and earth shifting to support the tether.

AWAKENING

NIGHT when I thought it was day.

Cold, but unnaturally so, or so said the daffodils that had pushed through the ground already, showing their brilliant yellow. Unlike the pinks and reds and yellows of the azaleas that bloomed in my neighbor's yard, the ones she fussed over and pruned, the ones I vomited into over the fence before I fell... fell while we were talking about summer vacation and watching each other's dogs: fell and never got up again.

Days?

Weeks?

Years since that day, the world cycling on without a care while I lay in my grave, cold and dank, trying to get out.

To get out.

Because I shouldn't be there... I shouldn't be in the ground.

Locked away.

Forgotten.

Because I am here and I can remember the way the sun kissed his hair while we sat on the deck, how the night sky looked when it was full of stars.

Because I can remember what it was like to laugh and walk and run, yes run, so I did run because I could and my legs could still carry me. They carried me right back to where I should be. Right back home.

Cold.

Unseasonably cold for April or May or whatever month it was. Killing my daffodils. Killing my follower that would come up even if I wasn't there to see them.

So yellow. I want to touch one but I am afraid to ruin it. When I see my fingers in the moonlight, gnarled and discolored, bloody because I had been clawing, clawing, clawing at the lid of the grave, beating against the cement enclosure, kicking my way up through the dirt, dirt that fell into my eyes to blind me... dirt that slipped into my mouth and down my throat to choke. I was afraid to touch the daffodils, not because I didn't want to make them like me because they were already like me—dead and revived, awakened, denied rest. No, I didn't want to touch the daffodils because I would soil them with the dirt from my grave and the dirt was my own.

Happy.

Laughing.

Music in the night.

They were probably dancing, maybe watching a TV show, the kids might be playing a game and maybe cooking together in the kitchen, maybe...

A new car in the driveway.

A new car where mine used to be.

They were probably loving anew.

The wind guided my steps and for that I was thankful because it meant I didn't have to think about it anymore, didn't have to find my way back to a place I didn't want to return.

But here I am.

The ground welcomed me back, kissed my skin as it peeled and left memories behind, let me pull its blanket over myself like an old friend.

POTENTIAL

ANGER BOILED down to complacency and it was quiet about it.

He didn't know what to do with that.

Like wine reduced to a concentrated flavor, what had set his teeth on edge, made him feel like he was going crazy, the clattering and banging of what she had become he feared would drive him over the edge and out of the door, became a smaller thing, a manageable annoyance once he spied what she hid behind her back. Down home squeeze brought to knees before the thing he'd hoped would hold them, and it didn't take much imagination for him to see how she'd played with his insides, torn free what she wanted to taste right away and wasted the rest.

Impulsive.

Greedy.

He'd have to teach her how to dress them properly so she didn't spill.

Oh, but her knifework was divine.

Time.

Give it time.

She might be ready for the ball after all.

ILL-GOTTEN

IT WAS hot and musty in the club even before the show got started. The air was thick, almost like you could see it hanging in front of you like wool, and Will had to stop himself from reaching out to touch it. He was surprised they would even let that many people in the place—it had to be some kind of violation to have wall-to-wall standing room only events in the old, single-stage bar, but it happened every week, and nobody said anything. They would when the floor caved in. There'd be a whole lot of shit to say when that happened.

Will didn't intend to be there for that, even if Mack indulged him a little, let him have more time before they had to run.

If... but that was a pipedream.

Will knew better.

Michelle, Renee, and Tip were nearby; Will had told them to stay close, kept reminding them about it like they were little kids on a playdate and he was the weary parent acquiescing to a detour in the park. That's kind of how he felt, truth be told. He liked them all right; there wasn't anything wrong with them, unless you wanted to call Tip out on his wigger shit, pull his hat off and let the lights hit that blond crown. There was money in his low hanging jeans, trust fund money that he didn't want the others to know about, but Will did. Will knew everything about him and the girls—he had known everything about every single one of them. Mack made sure he did in case he needed to make something happen.

Keep that in your back pocket, he'd said. Old gangster shit. Will's back pocket was full of all kinds of things now.

Did they even say 'wigger' anymore or was that from another life, another jump, some other blood stuck between him and Mack, or beyond, one that left behind remnants of shit that wouldn't mean anything to anyone who came after? Will didn't know and didn't have time to figure it out. Something big was coming if he could make the cards bump. The last run was a set up for him. Will had to make it count.

The beat was manufactured, muffled bass and what sounded like whispering, nothing like the music with live instruments that his grandfather used to play around the house. Will thought the 80s were bad... watered down, Jheri-curled whining that it was, and the 90s with passable slow music poisoned by sex-fueled lyrics, but this? This was on another level. He wished Mack hadn't come to him in his dreams, hadn't demanded his service, hadn't bothered with him at all. He didn't even know how to use the wormhole he had reached through to fuck with Will—Mack only knew that he *could* do it, so he did. Mack would keep on doing it until he got what he wanted and though Will tried his best not to think about how many people would get tapped for the job if he couldn't deliver—how many had already tried and failed—he couldn't stop his mind from going there, drawn to the thought like a beacon. Their eyes. Something inside him wanted to count the eyes of the ones who came and went, but Will shook the thought away. No more. Will was determined to make it stop... that night.

Michelle and Tip were dancing close, sparks flying between them, and Will wondered why they didn't just fuck already—leave the dancefloor and do the deed. They might not have the chance to after this—none of the others who had taken the ride with him ever got the chance to do anything but spill their blood on the asphalt and die. Will didn't have any reason to believe it would be any different for them either, and in the end, that didn't really matter. He only hoped that Mack knew why it had to be done and that he was right about it. After seeing what happened to the ones who had tried before, Will knew he only had one more shot —there would be no time to even take a breath after meeting the breach this time.

He was in his head.

Will was stuck in his head, and he knew he shouldn't be. Worrying about what had happened or not happened was a mistake. It would make him slow, sluggish, nostalgic for something that was never his to mourn. But still, he had seen all of their faces, ignorance and youthful optimism coloring their expressions the way it should color his but would not... not ever again.

Will had seen their faces as flesh separated from muscle, skulls gleaming in the cold, fluorescent light under an inky sky.

He had seen them in his dreams. He had watched as their mouths gaped, wishing them away, their swift passage his only desire. And even though Will didn't want to, he remembered.

He remembered them all.

When the man bumped into him near the bar, bodies packed so tight he couldn't help but do so, Will didn't hear what he said in response, and that was good. The words the man would have uttered might have helped Will figure out what decade he was in—at the very least, maybe even the actual year, but knowing how to respond might be a challenge. A misstep would make him stand out. Overthinking would bring on that misstep, so he didn't. He didn't look at the man either, for fear that he might stare. Will couldn't afford that, didn't have time for the problem that might come from it. Instead, he reminded himself that he belonged in that time and place. It was his, regardless of what Mack had shown him. He was himself and he was right where he was supposed to be.

Except that he couldn't be sure anymore, not when he could find an onyx pinky ring next to a pick with a fist for a handle on the nightstand where his cell phone charged. No, he couldn't be sure of anything anymore.

Biggie Smalls was asking for one more chance but that didn't mean anything; the greats play forever. KRS-One had just been booming through the speakers with a track from a decade before Biggie's hit; yeah, some shit is immortal. But Biggie coming through the speakers gave Will a starting point, one that made him feel even more confident that this time he could pull it off.

Because no one else had been able to do that yet.

If they had, what would he be doing now? Will knew it was foolish to think about that, to worry about what might have been, but he couldn't help it. Would he be across the country like he had planned when he thought he had some say about what came next? Would he have been travelling the world, maybe have gotten married and seen the sights with his wife? Would his mother still be alive if the dreams hadn't come... if Mack or one of the others had done what they set out to do and left him out of it? This was the question he hated most, because he knew the answer. Part of him wanted to kill Mack, even though he knew that was as ridiculous as threatening a corpse in a casket. But still, it's what he would do if it were possible. And who knows? None of what was going on—what had *been* going on since Mack had shown him everything—should be possible. So maybe, just maybe, there was a way to kill that motherfucker before Will sliced his own throat. Because that was what the other part of him wanted to do: kill himself, remove himself from the game-board: lights out. It was only right that he do so after what he was planning to let happen to Michelle and Renee and Tip. He would think of his mother when he did it too, would make sure he conjured up her dying eyes to stare at him while he breathed his last breath. He'd hope she knew it was for her, even though she would never have wanted it to happen. But it was the right thing to do, and he was a good boy, after all. If there was anyone watching, anyone who cared about penance in any real way, Will would be able to do that for her.

Like a fly on the wall, Will had been disturbed from a dreamless sleep and brought into a room that existed in a time long before his own. He was made to listen as Mack and his partner talked about things Will didn't understand. Will recognized Mack from an old photo album—a cousin; his mother's granduncle's son or something like that. He had been wearing what could only be described as a zoot suit in the picture Will saw, pinstriped and replete with a chain dangling from hip to knee. The picture showed him standing with three other people—two women, one man—whose names Will's mother did not know. They weren't written on the back in his grandmother's neat cursive either. Only the year—1955, no month, no day—and 'Friends', as she had labeled them, was scrawled there. 'Friends', and that is how they would stay in perpetuity, at least in his family's records. Will hadn't seen the picture a lot; it wasn't one that sat on their mantle, so he wasn't sure if the man in the room with

69

Mack was one of the two in the picture as well, but that wasn't what was forefront in his mind when he came to grips with who he was seeing.

He knew immediately that it wasn't a dream. He also understood, with all clarity, that this was the fork in the road.

"I mean, the first Negro talkie was shot here," the other man said.

"The what?"

"The first Negro movie with sound... it was shot right here."

"What?"

Will's long-lost cousin looked irritated, and instantly Will knew that sometimes the other man got on Mack's nerves talking about random shit. Mack sent the other man every signal he could to hurry things up. He looked at his watch, frowned over the time, pulled his eyes away to stare daggers at the other, then checked his watch again for good measure. When Mack spoke again, he was exasperated... beyond frustrated.

"What are you talking about, Carl?"

"Yeah," Carl said, stuffing his mouth with corn nuts, crunching them with his back teeth so loudly it could have made the bum in the corner stir, "Oscar Micheaux did it. Shot it right downtown."

Carl pointed toward the entrance they had used to get into the alley, and Will knew they had entered that way many times over many years. The entrance was in the direction of the George Washington Bridge that connected New Jersey and New York through Fort Lee and Manhattan. Will peered through the entrance to look at the sliver of sky he could see, but then Carl switched angles abruptly to point in the other direction.

"Or, no... I think it was that way. Wait... I'm screwed up," he said as he shifted his attention to the original direction he had pointed in again, a question on his lips.

"None of this shit would have been here then, so I'm all turned around, Mack, but it was here, that's for sure. Right here in Fort —"

"Nobody gives a shit about some old movie that was shot here!"

Will knew Mack didn't mean to yell as loud as he did—he could sense his cousin's thoughts. The idea of that telepathic connection was so disconcerting, it made Will dizzy. But it was real. Will knew that Mack hadn't meant to yell like that not because he didn't want to hurt Carl's feelings, but because of the bum in the room. Mack didn't want to have to deal with another surprise. Will had the distinct impression that there had been many surprises along the way already.

"It's history, Mack. It's important."

"Not to me, and it shouldn't be important to you... not if you know what's good for you."

He'd done it.

He'd threatened his best friend.

Will could feel the man's consternation, understanding context that he shouldn't. It had taken 20 years to get to that point and both men knew nothing good would come of it.

"It *better* mean something to *you*," Carl said as he stood to his full six feet, "if you know what's good for *you*."

Carl was imposing and he knew it. Mack tried to glower back but his heart wasn't in it. Carl knew that too.

"Carl...?" Mack said, unpuffing his chest, hoping that would be enough to cool things down, "what are you going on about? We need to get a move on—we don't have time to fool around with —"

"*The Exile*—that was the name of it," Carl continued as if he hadn't heard Mack talking and while that made Mack angry, he knew there wasn't anything he could do about it.

He already made the mistake of trying to use his weight to force Carl into doing something once and it was like running up against a brick wall. He wasn't interested in being repositioned like a child again, so he waited him out.

When Carl sat back down on an upended milk crate, Mack was relieved. Will knew all of this like he knew his own name.

"Made it back in 1931," Carl continued, the southern drawl of his people taking root in his pace, if not his pronunciation. "It's about a cowpoke who falls in love with a city girl, something like that. She's rich and wants to open a club or whatever they used to call it... a speakeasy, yeah. Anyway, they—"

"Carl!" Will saw Mack tense as if he expected the interruption to earn him one on the chin, but it was a chance he thought he had to take.

"History is *important*, Mack," Carl said, his eyes trained on his friend in a way that made him look soulless.

Mack's jaw worked, his teeth were grinding into powder as they sawed their way down to the gum. But Carl kept on.

"It's the ignorant who can't see that, and they will always be in the dark. As much as you come and go, you should care what goes on in between."

Mack's skin felt hot and Will felt flush too, especially when Carl looked away from him, ignoring the mounting anger on Mack's face to gaze thoughtfully at the high-rises peeking out from the mouth of the alley.

"She ain't mean us no harm," Carl said mournfully, looking at his calloused hands lying limp in his lap, "not at first. But we couldn't let well enough alone, could we? We just had to go, had to see. Once we caught a whiff of what smelled good, we had to have it. But it was hers and we shoulda left well enough alone."

"Carl," Mack started, but Carl kept talking.

"Ain't supposed to do folks like that. I knowed it and you did too. But it called to us like a bitch in heat, ain't it? I couldn'ta said no even if I tried. Be careful, pap. Be careful what you ask for, 'cause them roots'll get you."

"Carl," Mack tried again and this time the man looked at him with solemn eyes, "You's just tired, that's all. Just tell me where you put it and I'll get it back for us. We'll be livin' high on the hog uptown. Get us some dancin' girls to warm our beds. Come on, man, just tell me."

Carl's laugh came from deep in his chest and started slowly, bubbling up, building on itself as it rose to the surface. Mack didn't much like that—it made the hairs on his neck stand on end. Will could feel Mack's resolve cracking.

"What's so damn funny, man? Look," Mack said, shooting a glance around the room before lowering his voice, "we gotta get that shit before somebody else does, ok? It's *ours*. *We* did the work for it, not some, some bum whose gonna find it and run off."

Mack pointed at the man on the floor but Carl did not look at him.

"It's ours, man. Let's get what's coming to us."

Carl's laughter roared in the dilapidated room and a mix of emotions danced across Mack's face. Will could see that Mack was contemplating striking him; the tension in his body was as readable as words written on a page. But Carl didn't notice. He wheezed, and even though his chest ached, he took a deep breath, trying to take in enough air to speak. It was harder to do than before; Carl's breath grew labored and shallow as he deteriorated before Mack's eyes.

"Oh, we'll get what's coming to us... no matter how long it takes, we'll get it." It hurt... Will could see that everything hurt the man now, even though he had appeared strong moments before.

"Yes!" Carl said animatedly, his furrowed brow releasing

as Carl spoke the words, misreading the message and thinking his friend was coming around. "That's right, my man. We will get what's coming for us, that's for damn sure. Just tell me where you put it and I'll get it *for* us."

Carl nodded, still laughing. Mack was almost jumping up in down, his excitement was so complete.

"It's time."

"It is, man. It's long overdue, I'd say. But you know what, you're always right on time."

Carl stopped laughing abruptly and looked at the man he had called friend once upon a time. Disdain colored his features. His lips curled into a snarl before he spoke again.

"It's time to pay the piper, Mack."

Carl coughed and it sounded like the effort split his lungs apart.

Mack deflated as Will stared on incredulously. Mack didn't notice what was happening in front of him, didn't see what Carl was going through. Instead, he punched at the air in frustration, expending the anger and pent-up energy that had gathered in his joints as he coaxed Carl out. Mack wondered if his friend had grown senile waiting in that place. Was there really a screw loose like his own mama had thought there had been? Mack had never wondered before, but the prospect was too hard to ignore now.

"... can't just go on like we don't have to. We owe, and they gonna collect."

Carl had been talking but Mack hadn't been listening. He wasn't listening when he cut in either, not really. All he knew was that this—all of it—was bullshit.

"Are you calling me stupid, Carl? Huh?"

Mack's voice was loud but he didn't care. Not even his mama called him stupid, and he wasn't going to stand there and take that kind of guff from someone who hadn't even finished the 6th grade.

"I may not know whether I'm coming or going most of the time, but that don't mean I'm stupid. Are you saying I don't have no sense —"

And then it hit him—Will could see understanding dawning on Mack's face. It was a terrifying sight.

"Christ, I *have* been stupid," Mack said, in awe. "Dumber than a doornail, in fact. 1931, you say," he whispered, and Will felt like he could see lights dancing in his eyes. "The year the bridge went up."

Carl nodded and Will could tell that he was pleased with Mack for the first time in he didn't know how long. "I put it where the first Negro sound movie was made by the biggest Negro movie maker there had ever been, at least at that time. I'm sure you've seen bigger now. Me? I'll never get up from here, won't be here when you get back neither, and that's ok. Something that hard to have ain't for me no way, I guess."

Carl looked beyond Mack at the bum on the floor and Will followed his gaze. He almost screamed out loud when he saw the man's countenance in two place—animated in one and stone dead in the other. Will looked back at Carl quickly, feeling seen.

"That movie... the bridge... man, it's brilliant," Mack gushed, oblivious to all else. "How did you even *think* of that?"

Carl ignored Mack as he marveled over how intricate the plan had been, all the while trying not to let the admission that he would never have figured it out on his own leave his lips. Instead, Carl mused like an old man sitting in a rocking chair on a porch before a setting sun. He nodded in the direction of the George Washington Bridge.

"That's the world's very first two-level suspension bridge right there, did you know that? Went up the same year Micheaux did his thing. To me, can't be one without the other." Carl kept talking, his eyes landing on the bum's body reverently, his own bag of bones on the floor where it fell. "Why'd I do that? Because history is important, Mack. It's everything."

Carl leaned in and for a second Will wondered if he was about to slug Mack after all. But instead he said, low so nobody could hear,

"Find Metropolitan Studios and you finds the money."

When Will had woken up in bed the next morning, he had questions. When did the dream take place? It couldn't have been 1931, because they were talking about that year as though it had been in the past. Not in 1955 like the date on the back of the picture either—the man in the picture with Mack had been sporting a pompadour and there was not even the suggestion of one on Carl's head, though he might not have been in the picture at all—that was a possibility Will couldn't afford to forget. But something about Carl seemed more modern than that. Somehow, he seemed more wizened than Mack, more aware. He spoke of history and how important it was and Mack didn't seem interested in that at all. They were two different people, sure, but Will couldn't help but wonder if it was more than just different interests that stood out. Will wondered if the difference was deeper, more experienced, more grounded…generational.

He didn't have long to think about it.

Every night after the first one, a different dream came to Will. His vantage point was always somewhere in the room where they couldn't see him, but he was still part of the action. Will may have called them dreams but that was only because he didn't have another word to describe them, but he knew they were more than that. He knew that right away and didn't have time to let it frighten him. There was an urgency to them, a buildup he could feel in his very bones. Will needed to pay attention to what was happening in that weird state because not doing so might be the mistake he couldn't take back.

Tired man in checkered pants with cuffs that rode high off his shoes, his white sweater vest tight against his flat stomach walking across in the pedestrian path, crossing the bridge with the city lights of Manhattan's upper west side illuminating the sky behind him.

Afroed girl in a yellow tube top and brown and gold striped bell-bottoms riding in the back of a car, eyes wide in the dark of night.

Teenager in stone-washed jeans cuffed at the ankles but otherwise ballooned around his skinny lower half, skulking, trying to stick to the shadows once the cliff presented itself, almost like he would rather scale the rockface than pay the toll.

Man with a hightop fade and a gold herringbone chain that caught the light driving a black Ford Escort that had seen better days at top speed over the last joint that connected the bridge to asphalt, where it swapped suspension for firm, hard ground... a man who looked suspiciously like Will himself.

All of them, their friends, every last one compressed against the air before crossing properly into New Jersey, their bones broken, crushed, ground against something unseen in that nowhere land between states, dying without a home. *If* they had truly died. Will couldn't tell because before he could make himself look at the gore, the utter mutilation, they were gone, wiped away, like they never existed. No blood, no entrails, no bone. Just nothing. And then he would wake up in a bed soaked through with sweat and a promise on the air that he too would suffer the same fate if he didn't figure out a way.

"Hey man, we gotta go," Will heard himself say to Tip, his lips close enough to touch the man's ear. He didn't remember crossing the room and going out onto the dance floor to break up the love fest but there he was. He could see the disappointment on Tip's face but didn't stay long enough for the man to think he could ask for more time. They all knew they had to go, that being at the show was just to have an alibi if they needed one. Will hadn't told them everything, hadn't mentioned the dreams to anyone at all because they seemed so off the wall, but they knew there was something big at the end of the bridge, over there in Fort Lee, if they could just find it. But they had to go that night—not during the day, not some other time... *that night*. The prospect of a big haul kept their mouths closed, which Will had counted on. He hated himself for what he had done and what he was about to do, but there was no time to wallow in that either.

It was time.

The dancers came out hot, bouncing so energetically the makeshift platform buckled and threatened to break. Will wondered if the idea he'd had about the floor caving in had been some kind of premonition. There was yelling in his ears too. It had been coming to him here and there since the last dream two nights before. But Will assumed it was just his conscious trying to get hold of him for once, to make him change course and do something else. But his mother was dead because of the dreams and what Mack wanted him to find. She'd tried to stop him and he'd steamrolled over her a few jumps ago, and he owed. He couldn't remember how long it had been and that drove Will crazy, so he focused on finishing since that was the only thing he could do. There was no turning back, even if Carl's voice, deep and rich, boomed, "No!" in concert with every other step Will took.

He needed the dreams to stop.

He needed to finish this for his mother.

He needed to find what Mack wanted him to find.

"But where *exactly* are we headed?" Tip asked from the back seat. They were speeding across the George Washington Bridge and Tip's arm was curled around Michelle. Will was happy for him. She was into him—Tip didn't know that yet—he only hoped it was true—but she was. They probably wouldn't ever be able to do anything other than this—hug in the back seat of a cramped car—but at least they'd have that. Michelle's friend Renee had been quiet all night. She was supposed to be there to hang out with Will while Michelle and Tip figured out what they were going to get into, but she and Will had barely spoken two words to each other all night and that was ok, because it didn't matter if they spoke or not—she was supposed to be there because she was always there, her or someone like her. They all were. And that was ok too. In the end, everything would be.

Will answered the question, thought it was only right. After all, he could already feel the fillings in his teeth wrenching away from the enamel, struggling to get out, stretching, drawing, reaching toward something outside the car as if summoned by a magnet. Soon he'd see the flesh from Renee's face pull away from her skull, he'd watch Tip's eyes pop from their sockets as they followed the same yearning his fillings had. He'd hear the audible slaps their flesh would make as it hit the glass that would be pulsing by then, in and out, in and out, like a heartbeat, before it became liquid and overtook Tip's ruined eyes, submerging what was left in an impossible pool of metallic gray and sickly yellow.

Soon.

For now, only his teeth knew what was to come. And they began to ache.

Michelle was oddly quiet, her eyes reflecting the lights that illuminated the bridge like mirrors.

Will started, his voice gravelly, "We're going into Jersey to—"

"I can see that, man," Tip laughed and something inside Will didn't appreciate being the butt of the joke, just like his dear old cousin. "What I *don't* get is why we'd leave a bumpin' party right when it was startin' to get hot."

Tip let his hand dip lower than Michelle's shoulder to pet the flesh just above her breast. He thought he was really doing something, but she kept staring at Will with her dead eyes.

"To go to shitty-assed New Jersey."

Tip laughed, but nobody else did. It didn't stop him, though.

"What are we going to *do* in Jersey, pray tell?"

Pray tell? Will thought and fought the urge to shake his head. You could take the rich boy out of the country club, but you couldn't take the country club outta the rich boy.

"There's some money waiting for me there. At Metropolitan Studios."

Will told them that much because it didn't matter. They would never be able to stop him. They would never be able to tell anyone else either, not if his dreams were right.

"Money? *Just* money? Man..." Tip said, as if it were the most ridiculous reason to mess up an otherwise perfect night. "You shoulda just said something. We didn't need to drive all the way out here for some *money*. You know I got you. Somebody owe you or something?"

Will stayed silent, listening. He tasted blood in his mouth.

"Man, we coulda taken care of this some other time."

Tip looked over at Michelle, noting where his hand was and let the corner of his mouth raise in an anticipatory smile he probably thought was charming. He let his gaze linger as he continued,

"I coulda fronted you whatever it was if you needed it like that."

Tip was genuinely upset and Will could appreciate that. He thought about saying something to placate him but dug the tip of his tongue into the gaping hole one of his fillings had left instead.

"We're all gonna die," Michelle said, her monotone voice

filling the cabin as Tip ranted about how he thought there was jewelry or gold or other shit waiting for them out there in Jersey. He said a whole lot of things that didn't make a lot of sense but it was all background noise to Will. Will was entranced by Michelle's words and the faraway look in her eyes.

But he seemed to be the only one who heard her.

When he looked at Michelle, turning in his seat to face her, he noticed that one of her irises had detached and was crumpled over itself in a heap of brown.

Will turned back to the road and smiled. Blood stained his teeth.

"Wait. Will... man, did you say Metropolitan Studios?"

Will didn't trust his voice so he nodded.

"There *is* no Metropolitan Studios, dude." Tip laughed incredulously as he pulled Michelle closer. All Will heard was, 'Stupid idiot. Stupid nigger. Stupid ass.'

"What?" Will managed and spat blood onto the steering wheel. "What the fuck did you just say?"

"Yo, are you all right?" Tip asked, leaning forward to peer closer at Will and the bloody spit dripping down the center pad of the steering wheel. "Is your nose bleeding or something? I used to get nosebleeds all the ti —"

"What. The. Fuck. Did. You. Say?" Will's voice wasn't much more than a growl.

Tip sat back carefully, keeping his surprised eyes on the back of Will's head.

"I said the studios are gone," Tip hedged cautiously, all humor gone from his voice. "That place burned down a long time ago. Decades ago, man. Before our time. Been gone since the 50s, I think."

The lights on the bridge illuminated the cabin of the car like the searchlight of a helicopter and Michelle's eyes reflected it, shooting it at Will like laser beams.

All white.

All white.

No red.

No cars on this bridge because we're all dead, the voice in Will's head trilled.

Movie magic.

Dead magic.

He should have known…

…would have, but Mack would never believe.

And Michelle was laughing.

"Whoever told you they left money at the studio for you was pulling your leg. There's nothing left of the place."

Will didn't hear Tip tell him that he thought it was a park now, didn't notice when Michelle's voice cracked and broke, nor when she started hitting her head on the glass, thud thud thudding against it until it broke. He heard only Renee because she had started screaming, screaming like she had seen Hell through the split that was opening at the mouth of the bridge, screaming like doing so would save her from the jagged, gnashing teeth that waited inside. And then he heard Mack's voice, and he was screaming too.

I KNOW

When the board creaks I know.

Shadows playing with the moon, making finger puppets on the wall and yes, I know that it's him and not me, that it's him come for me because he loves to play even if he has no hands to do it with anymore.

Cold.

Cold as the ice that encased him, trapped him, blanketed him below, down under, deep in the frigid blue. It's like that outside when the board creaks, and I feel it. I feel it and I cover up, shield myself, tell the air, the clouds—whatever will listen—that I can creak too.

!

THE LIGHT. The light came on. The light came on and I am alone. The light came on and I am alone in the house, alone on the street, alone in this world. The light came on and I am alone in the house. Alone in the house.

Alone.

In.

The.

House.

Downstairs. The light came on downstairs. The light came on downstairs and that is my only way out. My only way out of the house is down the stairs, downstairs, where the light came on… where someone turned the light on.

Was the timer on?

When I go to visit my cousin and we sit on the lake for hours at a time, I sometimes set the timer to turn the lights on so people think I'm still home, still here, puttering around and watching TV. If they watched close enough they'd know that the timer comes on too late. Later than I would normally watch. Later than I would normally walk the house. It was too late, and they'd know that if they paid attention.

Was someone watching?

Had someone noticed me, my patterns, and what I do? Did they know I don't do anything, nothing at all, and I would be here if they wanted to come in, if they wanted to scare me, if they wanted to hurt me?

The light came on downstairs and I know the timer was off. I turned it off a few weeks back, after my last trip. I didn't catch anything. After all day, I didn't catch anything and I was tired, so I turned if off and went up to bed. Right?

Sure. Because if I hadn't, I'd have seen the light every night since then.

Unless I fell asleep before it came on.

Had I?

It came on late, too late, so I might have fallen asleep, been in Lalaland by the time it came on, still asleep when it went off. Could be. But I turned it off when I came home that day. I turned it off... I'm positive I did...

The light came on downstairs and I looked for the clock upstairs. I looked toward the darkened guest room because that was the only room I could see into from where I was standing near the top of the stairs. I couldn't move, couldn't walk to my bedroom to look at my cellphone, or check the time there because my feet were frozen. So I squinted as I searched the darkness of that room, trying to see the alarm clock with the red digital numbers. Is that a 6 or an 8? The numbers merged together beneath my meshing eyelashes, blurring, obscured. I squinted again. I raised a hand to shield my eyes, but in the end what did it matter? It didn't matter if it was either a 6 or an 8. Neither of those would be right. It would be early. Too early for the timer to turn on... the one that comes on late.

Too early.

The light came on downstairs and I back away from the stairs terrified of what comes next, terrified of making noise… terrified because I know I turned the timer off, just like I know it isn't 10 or 11 o'clock at night and, therefore, late. I know it is. I'm up too high and would break a leg if I tried to jump out of a window. I know that too. Someone was there, down there, in the kitchen or in the living room waiting for me to come down and say hello. I knew that much too. And if I said hello, I'd never be able to say goodbye again.

TRADITION

"Zettaidesu."

The sweat that had formed when he realized what they expected him to do, leaching from his skin to form pools that turned cold in the evening air, had spilled over his sparse eyebrows to drip into his eyes, stinging them. It was not a joke. In this day and time, in the midst of the 21st century when practices like these seemed antiquated and backwards —when the threat of such consequences seemed the stuff of legend, the reality of another time and place—they were really going to do it. He had laughed at first, wanting to be ahead of the joke, ready to take the slap on the wrist he would surely get for what they considered an indiscretion— something that he thought was less than what that son of a bitch had deserved —and walk out of the door. But his oyabun was there, and he was never out in the open. Kaito hadn't even seen the man more than twice in the six years he had been Yakuza. But he was there, waiting. It had been him who had handed Kaito the tanto that had apparently been passed down for four generations, an ancient looking thing with a wooden grip and tempered blade.

Kaito tried to stop himself from wondering how many times it had been put into service.

The sweat dripped onto the table, falling from his hair as if wet from a shower. He was shaking. He could see the hair moving above his eyes, his usually straight high-top fade weighed down by the heat of panic, strands dipping into view at the edges of his peripheral vision. He was trembling, wiggling free fat droplets of sweat. *His* sweat. His *fear*.

A grunt sounded from somewhere in the room; a noise that spoke of impatience, bordered on disgust. If the penalty for beating up their enemy's son, a man who had ogled his sister and had been a stranger to Kaito before war was waged, bore the knife, he feared what the disrespect of making his oyabun wait might be.

Fingers littered the floor. Kaito imagined he could see fingers all around him, mounds of them like so much dirt, as one returned to the soil in rot another lay atop it anew.

Fingers on the floor next to his shoe, expensive imported sneakers he wished he hadn't spent his money on.

Fingers on the chair behind him, cauterized by an unseen flame held by a phantom, nerves still twitching, writhing, responding to the pain.

Fingers on the table next to his sweaty palm wearing the ring he had taken from the man whose blood he spilled.

Ninkyō dantai they liked to call themselves—so-called chivalrous organizations. His snicker sounded loud in the room.

Kaito looked at the knife.

He looked at his finger, the scales he'd had tattooed there years ago seeming to glow under the strain.

Sweat dripped from his head to pool with the rest on the table.

"Dekimasen," Kaito whispered desperately, hating the tears that sprang from his eyes to join the sweat.

Akio was standing close enough to hear Kaito say he couldn't do it, close enough to see that he was crying. He wanted to help him, wanted to come to the aid of the junior leader who showed him kindness more often than not, but he was low man on the totem pole, a shatei, even lower than Kaito was. If he kept his head, Akio might be pulled up in rank after this, might even take Kaito's spot as wakashu and get trained to lead. He hated that he would be advancing on the back of his friend's misery but he knew all too well what the alternative was: if they saw him showing Kaito any sympathy, he might see the business side of the tanto as well.

"Dekim —" Kaito started again but heard the sharp voice of the man he had taken under his wing. Akio. Nothing more than a kid, really, but stepping up to be a man... now.

"Meiyo," Akio hissed and Kaito thought he might kill him one day for spouting off about honor when he was on his knees. That is if he didn't get an infection from the rusty blade or bleed out right there surrounded by underlings and overlords.

"Yubitsume," Akio said firmly, earning an appreciative nod from his oyabun.

Yes, Kaito decided. If he got out of that situation alive, he might relish pulling the blade across Akio's neck.

Kaito picked up the tanto, deciding it was better not to look at Akio lest he see the fear in his eyes. He raised the knife over his left hand, the blade catching the light as it waited to connect. It was sharp and that was good. Maybe he could avoid gangrene.

"Moushiwake gozaimasen. Kanben shite kudasai," Kaito said, begging for mercy when he knew none would be given, but doing it anyway because it was expected. He bowed again for the same reason, all the while repeating a manta in his head, one that was supposed to reassure him but that failed,

"Just the pinky… it's just the tip… just the pinky… it's just the tip…"

A white cloth lay on the table waiting to receive his finger. He would then wrap it up and present it to his oyabun in an act of contrition.

The white would be soiled, ruined forever.

The red of his blood would be so bright it would appear to glow.

Kaito thought he might be sick.

He raised the knife higher and thought of an old mystery he had once watched on television as he drove the blade down, his thoughts passing in slow motion as it cut through the air. It was a black and white affair, something from the '50s that his grandfather had turned on and promptly fallen asleep in front of. Ten fingers sat in a pile on the floor behind a closed door. There were no bodies and the door had not been locked but when the maid came into the room she found the digits there, ends still wet with blood. There had been no other way out of the room than that door and the maid swore no one had gone in or come out since the original ten had gathered there to drink, talk, do whatever it was they did in movies like that. The window was closed. There was a fire burning in the fireplace. The police had no idea where to look. Kaito wondered what kind of clue his finger might have given them if they found it, tattooed with the scales of a dragon, nail manicured and neat.

IT KILLED THE CAT

"I HEARD they do it twice a year, sometimes three. Whenever their schedules line up," Charlie had said, chewing absently on what Jun Bae didn't know. What Charlie said so casually would resonate in Jun Bae's mind, would echo there later as he realized he had overstepped, when he knew it was too late to save himself, but Charlie would never know it. When he heard the news Charlie still might not think of him, make the connection. The name would mean nothing to him or anyone else in their world. Jun Bae had effectively become 'JB' to everyone in the business, and by "the business" he meant the sleazy, picture-taking bastards he had cast his lot with; the ruiners of reputations; the demons who held the keys to happiness and sadness and would gladly give them up... for a price. Jun Bae adopted the moniker 'JB' instead of letting himself get saddled with June Bug. It had been eight years since he had started introducing himself that way and he still thought the former was a better look.

Mok Jun Bae, son to a professor and a dance instructor, brother to a seamstress.

Junie, friend to few but loyal to the ones who stuck around.

Jun Bae, boyfriend to none, lover only ever to one and that distinction he truly regretted.

JB, trespasser, rule breaker, son of a bitch.

Dead man, he reminded himself. *Don't forget that one.*

He didn't need to feel the barrel of a gun on the back of his neck to know he was a goner—the story was laid out before him in vivid color, full color bleed, centerfold.

He had seen too much.

He had seen it all.

He wouldn't be allowed to tell.

Charlie told him everything he wanted to know—it was like a love story, poetry, dew on rose petals—all that shit. It was exactly what someone like Jun Bae wanted to hear— exactly the type of thing he'd love to destroy, burn to the ground so that the ones who enjoyed it couldn't have it anymore. He was the *sasaeng* who went into the bathroom stall after a K-Pop star left to collect any urine they could find. He was the paparazzo who stood outside of schools hoping to catch a picture of a celebrity picking up their kids. Jun Bae was the combination of the most obsessed fans and the most unscrupulous photographers times 10. Freelancer, he liked to call himself, but the people he stalked had more colorful words to describe what he did for a living.

No one understood why he did what he did. He didn't have to—he had prospects. Mok Jun Bae had graduated magna cum laude from a top-ranked college, had companies reaching out to *him* to join their ranks, which was all but unheard of anymore. But he didn't want any of that—at least not yet. Junie's friends figured he'd join them in the mind-numbing grind of office work one day—figured he'd be their boss as soon as he got there, his foray into whatever he called what he was doing being considered self-exploration rather than fucking around. They assumed that Jun Bae, as the girl who'd let him make love to her knew him, would mature from the shy, inexperienced sophomore into the confident man he should be considering how broad his shoulders were, how gorgeous his eyes. And now he'd never get a chance.

Because JB liked this shit. All of it. He'd had a supermodel from London offer to blow him if he'd burn the pictures of her shooting up between her toes. An action star from Mumbai first threated to kick JB's ass then offered to set him up with a castmate if he would forget about the conversation he'd overheard between him and his cosmetologist about skin lightening. A K-Pop star tried to seduce him, offering him exclusive access to what was between his legs if he'd just delete the pictures of him at dinner with a male prostitute from Busan. And then there was the American actor's transgender fiasco... Jun Bae hadn't taken any of them up on their offers and not because he wasn't tempted. Truth was, he was tempted by many of them. But the money tempted him more than a one-night stand ever could, even with one of the most attractive people in the world.

Infinitely more.

Charlie told Jun Bae that they were meeting that night and it was bound to be good because they hadn't gotten the chance to get together in almost a year. He said he was sure that it would be hot, so many pictures to be taken, so many angles. Charlie said he wished he could go with him—actually looked like it pained him not to, and that should have made the alarms go off in Jun Bae's head, but it didn't. After all, this wasn't the first time he had heard of such a story; celebrities had whole networks in place so they could live normal lives. They took over Podunk towns, had supermarkets and movie theaters, post offices and gas stations—the same stuff every place has, only these towns weren't on the map. They could walk the streets and not worry about someone catching them looking less than runway ready. At least that was the rumor. Jun Bae, JB —hell, he didn't know who he was anymore—had never seen one of these created towns, but he could believe they existed. It made sense to him in the same way that whole neighborhoods could be formed around one ethnicity, a place where people could buy what they wanted, go where they wanted, be who they wanted because everyone else was just like them. Without places like that, JB was sure he'd have more work because the celebrities would lose their shit on a regular basis. He'd be rolling in it if that happened because behaving badly sold just as much as blurry sex pictures did.

Jun Bae had never been to one of these gatherings he'd heard rumors about, but he was game—of course he was... he was counting the money he'd make before he even snuck in, visions of the Brazilian underwear model doing a split for the Canadian rapper while the German director watched with his bottom lip clenched between his teeth, dancing in his head. It had been a while, Charlie said. They might be horny as hell, Jun Bae's mind supplied. He checked the battery life on his camera again, just to be sure.

The room was dark—dark leather furniture, huge oak bookshelves, dark green, dark brown, dark everywhere.

The light was dim.

The music was low—some kind of Egyptian trap music slowed down and reverbed in a way that wasn't unpleasant. He liked it; it drew him in. In fact, he was listening too closely, closer than he should have been, at the expense of everything else as he walked into the room, wondering who might have chosen this music to set the mood. The new Japanese heartthrob who split his time between his home country and Morocco? The American singer rumored to be engaged to the Malaysian model who was so sought after that even veteran outfits couldn't seem to book him?

Somewhere deep down inside Mok Jun Bae was disgusted with himself.

JB salivated.

The door closed behind him and Jun Bae jumped because he had closed that door himself ever so quietly only moments before. He had taken a few steps into the room, lured like a snake in a charmer's basket by the music, so rhythmic, enticed by the orgy he expected to find... the combination a promise of the perfect photo lingering in the air like incense. And yes, there was skin on skin and hands moving and bodies writhing in unison, but he didn't get to see it for long. It was just a distraction, one designed perfectly for him. While the hand that held the camera twitched, as his arm began its ascent toward his face to position the lens for the perfect shot, he had not noticed that someone had opened the door after him, had slipped into the room behind him, not until it was too late and the cold steel against his neck was cutting into his throat. They came for him then, money in hand, mouths open to kiss, leaving dollar bills in their wake—his pockets filled as they bit his skin to drink what flowed. Naked some, but that didn't matter anymore, not when someone kept cutting his neck, cutting and laughing, cutting and drinking. The sounds filled his ears as did the voices that followed, disembodied and fleeting as they paid to play.

Money in his pockets.

Money in his eyes.

Snap.

Snap.

Someone taking their own pictures from a perch unseen.

A glass filled from the fount of his neck and handed to the Brit wearing the blue paisley ascot.

The Nigerian actress laughed heartily at a joke that the

Scottish DJ was telling her, licking a finger that had been dipped in JB's blood.

Snap.

Mok Jun Bae wondered if they would accept his sincere apologies for his indiscretion.

Junie cried silent tears.

Jun Bae tried to scream but his vocal cords had already been destroyed.

JB smiled for his close-up.

BLIND

THEY DIDN'T SEE her when she listened to the reading, her eyes closing in rapture as the author spoke their words, revealed their truth... spoke of things that sat in her soul. They didn't see her then and they wouldn't see her later, when she listened to the call to action, leaned into her destiny, exactly the way she was encouraged to. They didn't see her—never saw her—but they would, and then they would know, then they would understand. They would see judgement on her face, years of it after enduring unnoticed. They would see, and never forget.

DOPPELGANGER

He would never let it happen again.

The man had slipped him the last time, disappeared in a sea of faces, another body among the throng. But not this time. Jace had followed him across three states, had stuck the shadows while he stood in the light. Jace had been everywhere he had gone for months, watching opportunities come and go, but he was determined to finish it this time. No more running. No more hunting.

Jace couldn't afford the alternative.

The man, the one who wore his face, had taken things that Jace knew he could never get back. The people in his life who would have believed him were gone. Many had died before the imposter had shown his face, but some were taken in, exploited, and killed by the man and his lies. They believed that he was who he said he was—who he looked to be, and really, who could blame them? The man looked like he did. Jace didn't have a twin brother, so when he said he was Jace himself, why wouldn't they believe him? And they paid for it. With their dying breaths, they paid handsomely.

His coach.

A colleague.

Jace was there to settle the score.

Jace was there to kill him.

He'd been following him ever since finding blood on the floor in his kitchen, blood he tracked around the house after stepping into it. How he'd gotten in, Jace didn't know but none of that mattered anymore. He saw the police pull up to his house ready to arrest him for the crimes the imposter had committed. He didn't stick around to see what happened next.

The man mingled with people day in and day out as if he hadn't left bodies in his wake. And Jace followed. Closely, but not close enough. Not close enough to wrap his hands around his throat. Until tonight.

And Jace was ready to settle the score.

The city lights were beautiful, red and amber hues back-lighting tall buildings, but Jace didn't have time to appreciate it. The knife he'd held in his waistband, the one that nearly sheared off a sliver of skin from his hip when he sat down without adjusting, had been brandished as he began moving in anticipation, moving without forethought—moving outside of himself, in spite of himself. Everything was heightened now, the chase was over and it was time for the showdown—the moment he had been looking for since the man, the fucking bastard had ruined his life. And he was ready, god, so fucking ready to do this thing, the cut out the cancer, then pluck out the eye and cut off the hand and whatever other biblical punishments he could think up. Because he deserved it.

The knife felt heavy in his sweaty palm.

The echo of his screams bounced off the walls of the alley in a cacophonous fury as he noted, with as much anger as there was confusion, that he was indeed alone.

AGREE TO DISAGREE

OUT OF A MOUTH that promised gifts so sweet, with garlic and wine, the notes were a delicacy, flesh supple, luscious: exquisite.

FAMILY PLOT

JONAH CAME to the cemetery with his family. He dropped flowers around like he was spreading birdseed, said no prayers, and dawdled when it was time to go. Something always caught his eye—a funny name (Penelope sometimes, but Gertrude at others), or a date that seemed older than time itself. His parents would call him along, hurry him, admonish him for lagging behind. Hands reached out unseen, pressing him forward, helping him on his way with a pat on the bottom or two for good measure. It made him giggle when someone ruffled his hair or another lifted him off his feet, made him feel like he was walking on air. At least, it did when he was young. But they'd known enough to stop when he no longer threw the flowers, to visit from afar when he stayed near his mother, his father long gone.

They bid silent luck to him and his intended when he brought her by to meet the family.

They mourned with him and wrapped their arms around his mother when they said their final goodbyes.

He brought flowers and placed them on every stone with care.

He had a bench installed near his mother so he could visit with her.

There were picnics and happy times when he shared stories of what was happening on their street, their neighborhood, their lives. But then his back rounded and his legs failed and he only came once, twice, three more times, hair thinning more with each autumn.

The child who came to tell them where he was stood tall. She was 35 and had children of her own, she said. Their grands and great-grands—faces they had never seen. He was gone, she said, and wouldn't be back there. Neither would she, not to sit before their graves, not to visit as she had at his knee... at least not for a long time. He and her mother were elsewhere, laid to rest in some town none of them knew, and she thought that meant they couldn't find him, that they had lost him forever. She was sad for them, grieved their loss of company for them as she sat on that bench, her father's bench, for the last time. But when she spoke, there was music in her voice—his favorite song he said, as he gazed upon his daughter's face. Jonah smoothed her hair even though they told him not to, and when she felt the unexpected warmth on the crisp autumn air, she smiled.

THE ROOM

"IT WAS COMING FROM OVER THERE," the maid said, though she didn't really need to. Anyone standing in the hallway could have figured that out—maybe even anyone who happened to be in their rooms. If they were smart, and some of them were, they would have stayed inside, keeping the drywall and insulation between them and whatever was making that godawful noise. Some had done exactly that— had maybe even slept through all the commotion, though there was little chance of that. But others, a small few but still some, had cracked their doors and peered out to see what they could see. There was nothing *to* see, as it turned out, but what they heard would play in their dreams over and over, for the rest of their lives.

The hotel manager blew past the maid, hardly even seeing her. He had wondered why she hadn't opened the door herself with the passkey she used to get access to clean, wondered how much this was going to cost him in noise complaint allocations and online reviews, wondered how many people it would take to clean up whatever the hell was going on in there—thought about all of this while he was in the elevator heading up to the 5th floor where, apparently, all hell had broken loose, but when the doors opened and he stepped into the hallway lucid thought was replaced by all-encompassing noise. His body moved toward it of its own volition even though some small part of his mind tried its best to make him stop walking, back up, retreat into the safety of the elevator and let it take him away from there. But he kept moving, moving toward the maid, rounding the corner where she stood looking as if she might urinate on herself, and heading toward the room.

Room 515.

It was loud.

It was so very loud, like someone was being killed inside. And not just killed—gutted, eviscerated, innards pulled out through the tiniest hole in the stomach, skewered with something... maybe the free pen they left on the desks, the ones with the hotel logo on it... small, small so it could hurt that much more. His mind, never particularly creative before, provided him images of a rounded ballpoint protruding from something pink and tubular and bloody, black ink spilling out over it, mixing with the red of the blood, shining in the fluorescent light of the room.

Those bright, daylight bulbs that he hated so much.

He had told the board not to invest in those, said they were unnatural, accosting to the eye, made the place feel more like a hospital. An uncharitable laugh coughed out of his mouth, and he wished he could have bitten back, could have swallowed it down before it fell all the way out into the air and into the memory of anyone listening, anyone who might recount the story of what happened at the Mandrake Hotel that day—anyone who might remember the callous manager laughing dismissively about what might be happening in Room 515. But that's not what he was doing—it wasn't what he was doing at all. He was laughing, true, he couldn't deny that, but not because anything struck him as funny. No, he was laughing because the fluorescent lights he had cautioned them against, the ones that were probably incredibly bright against what had to be a massacre, were perfectly utilitarian now, just as they would be in a morgue.

The manager held his passkey, pulling it from his hip, unravelling the reel as far as it would go, watching the cord grow taut, but it wasn't far enough. Self-preservation had made him stand back from the door, further back than would allow the sensor to read the card. He cursed as he watched his fingers tremble. He had pushed for this too, but the board decided to put upgrading their access system on the backburner and refurbished the restaurant instead. That meant instead of holding the card up and watching the pretty red light turn green, he couldn't get into the room without swiping his card in the card reader and that meant he had to get close—much closer than he was now, much closer than he was comfortable with. At least the people in the restaurant could enjoy their shitty food in button-tufted chairs.

He hesitated.

Why wasn't security trying the door? Isn't that what they were supposed to do in situations like this? Unlock the door and go in first? Break the damned thing down if they couldn't get in any other way? Surely they were supposed to do something more than breathe down his neck... right?

Everyone was looking at him.

He was too far from the door.

The hand holding the badge shook. The arm of the hand holding badge did too. Everything on him shook—he felt sure he looked like a kid's cartoon, knees knocking as he stood there in front of Room 515 doing absolutely nothing to help the woman inside, and she was screaming, screaming so loud, dear God she was screaming like she was being mutilated.

The hotel manager took a deep breath, cursing himself for not leaving the company like he had thought about doing the year before, signing on with one of the larger conglomerates in the city—the ones who didn't know your name but gave you a bonus every year just the same. He took a step forward, hoping that would be enough to reach, wishing he hadn't come in that day, that he had rolled over and hit snooze, that his car had broken down.

No.

Not far enough.

He took another step and hoped no one heard him gulp.

He swiped the card.

The light turned green.

Security did their job, pushing into the room before he had the chance to take another step, and he was more relieved than he cared to admit. As they moved past him armed with nothing more than their size, the hotel manager realized how much of a farce the whole thing was. There were no weapons, no handcuffs, one of them wasn't even taller than he was. They just had muscle. And that wouldn't be enough to protect them against someone who could make a woman scream like that.

And they hadn't called the police yet.

Not yet because the description he had been given at first only said that someone was yelling. That could have been anything—a party that moved from the bar to the bedroom, wild sex, the television. He had seen it all. But as the first guard dispatched made his way toward the elevator, another call came in about the noise, and then another. The hotel manager hadn't decided to come along as much as he had been ushered along, recruited, disturbed from his coffee and pleasant conversation with the bellhop. So he hadn't had the chance to make the call, not yet.

He should have called when they were in the elevator.

He should have called when they stepped onto the floor.

He should have called..

The room was empty.

He would have called out to the guards if his feet hadn't propelled him backwards first, his body acting on instinct. It would have been futile anyway—he knew they hadn't disappeared into another room and out of view. They couldn't have—not that quickly. Besides, he saw. He would never get the chance to tell anyone that, but he did. One of them walked into a nightclub where all the women looked like Juanita Boisseau and Cab's swing was keen. The other one took the hand of a goddess in blue whose feet didn't touch the floor.

Everyone was looking at him.

The maid.

The nosy guests.

Waiting...

for him to do...

something.

The white rug was too bright when the fluorescent daylight bulbs were on full bore: he was right about that. The blood pooling at the top of his thin mustache, that stupid little thing he had insisted upon keeping even though it made him look ridiculous, seemed entirely too red as it shined in the light. What did they think he should do about that?

IT'S THE LITTLE THINGS

He had time to wonder if the switch downstairs was stuck in that halfway position, neither on nor off—stuck right in the middle just waiting for the right jostling to move it. He had done that before—not turned the switch off all the way and it popping back into place and he didn't know why. It could have been the house settling or someone walking heavily on the floor above: anything could have created enough of a thump to make the switch pick a side. Only there wasn't anyone else in the house this time—no one to jump around on the floor above and bang the ceiling to shake the switch into action.

It was just him.

He had enough time to think about that, the fact that he was home alone. It was a rare occurrence these days—with school being out and his wife working from home, there was always someone else around, beating him to the room he had planned to claim to watch TV or using the last of the cheese and forgetting to write it on the grocery list. When the kids went to their friends' houses for sleepovers and his wife and her girlfriends decided that their girls time was long overdue, he couldn't believe his luck. His wife had asked him if he was going to be lonely at home all by himself and for a moment he thought she might change her plans to have a date night with him instead. And that would have been fine too, but he was going to stay up and wait for her to come home anyway, add a part two to the evening. He wanted her to have a part one doing whatever she wanted to do and he wanted one too—one that was just him and an action movie playing as loud as he wanted it; him with a cold one and some explosions, popcorn and bad acting. He wanted to be alone in the house for the first time in what seemed like years.

His wife of 15 years, love of his life, and mother of their kids, understood.

So, out she went with her friends and out he went to drop off the kids. He expected the kids to stay up half the night doing the same thing he was doing—watching loud movies and loving every minute of them. One would be watching horror movies and the other action. None of them would get any sleep. But he'd deal with the sleep deprivation tomorrow. Tonight was his.

He had time to remember that the microwave would beep soon to remind him that his butter was ready: melted perfection just waiting to kiss the popcorn he had already made. He also wondered if the fan on the stove would come on again while he was standing there, stuck, glued in place. That's what it had done when he came into the house after dropping the kids off—just turned on for no reason. He thought it too was in that weird middle position—the knob precariously there in limbo. He wondered who had cooked last and left it like that. Probably his daughter. She was good for that, was always cooking, always filling the sink with dirty dishes. It was probably her. His son rarely turned the fan on at all, even when the room was filling with smoke.

He checked, but no. The knob was in the off position, pointing straight up, just like it was supposed to be. Yet it was on.

Electrical problem. It had to be that. First the stove and now the light switch. He would definitely have to call someone out to fix it—he had time to remember thinking he might not be able to fix the stove on his own when he saw it earlier, had time to wonder how much that little visit would cost. One burner had been running hot recently, burning up all the food, even when it was set to 2 or 3. And now the fan was having problems.

He had time to remind himself to send an email to his account so that he didn't forget. Had time to wonder if he'd really get the chance to do that or if this was just his brain trying to save itself because time... time was for someone else to worry about, for someone else to spend, because his was up.

It was dark outside; night had fallen while he was prepping for his time alone: renting the movie, grabbing the beer, popping the popcorn. He had turned the light on as he made his way up the steps because the stairwell was darker than it had been when he had left it and he didn't want to run the risk of tripping over something the kids had left out—the hoodie he saw balled into a wad on the floor near at the bottom of the stairs was chief in his mind, but there could be more stuff left around that he didn't remember. It was smart, he thought—turning on the light like that. His father had once fallen off the last step because his foot twisted on the face of some toy. He could remember the way his father's glasses had slid across the floor, how mad he was to find himself on his knees. It probably hurt too, but his father had never said anything about that.

He didn't feel like taking a detour to that pain if he could help it.

He had time to wish he hadn't set himself up in the basement, the place that had ceased to be his as soon as the kids got old enough to commandeer it, the place he hardly even went into anymore except to check that the sump pump was working and that the furnace wasn't blocked by anything.

He had time to wish he had brought the butter down with everything else even though he knew he would have dropped something if he had tried.

Stuck in the middle... the switch. Curious.

He had time to consider reaching for it, time to think about taking steps toward it to change its position... time to realize he'd never make it, not with legs that no longer seemed under his control or a mind that knew, was absolutely certain, he couldn't change it—would never be allowed to. It was finished and as much as he wanted it to, time would never deign to wait for him.

Quiet.

So very quiet.

He had time to wish he wasn't alone in the house, so very alone, but was grateful that it was him who was standing in the stairway, halfway between floors, in the sudden darkness, because he didn't want his family to see what he saw when the light went off.

A WARM FALL DAY

"You know you shouldn't just stare at people's houses like that."

Brendan's voice pulled Jim back into the world, jolted him out of whatever reverie he had been in. He jumped unconsciously as though Brendan had shouted in his ear.

"What?" Jim asked and was surprised to find his voice hoarse. He cleared his throat, fought the urge to bring his hand up to rub at his neck.

"I said what if someone did that to you—stared at our house like that—and you caught them? You'd be more than a little pissed, don't you think? Especially with the face you had on just now."

Jim looked at Brendan with confusion dancing in his eyes. He let himself be led away from the front of the modified bungalow and over to the decidedly less conspicuous side of the house where the odd sloping roof met the edge of the porch railing. There were fewer windows there and that was probably good because Jim was still staring at the house, his lips slightly parted in that weird way he affected when he was surprised, taken aback, knocked off-kilter. He let

Brendan move him where he wanted because Jim wasn't sure if he could do it himself. His legs felt like they were pinned in place, heavy like the soles of his shoes were lined with cement that had begun to harden as he stood in front of the house, the brown house that looked like a man tilting his head to the side, dipping his fedora, the window not hidden beneath the would-be brim threatening to wink at Jim while he looked. He thought that if it winked, if someone went into that room and rolled down the shade at that precise moment, he might faint dead away. As curious as that idea was, as unbidden and fantastical as that train of thought seemed, what bothered Jim most was the cold terror that snaked up his neck at the thought of what would happen to Brendan then.

"Come on," Brendan said good-naturedly, but Jim knew that tone and it was anything but. Brendan's happy go lucky, 'what—are—you—doing—silly' lilt really meant, 'Get your shit together, Jim. You're embarrassing me,' and Jim supposed he was. Or would. If not today, then one day when he didn't walk quite as fast as his decades younger partner or when the break he ended up taking on a park bench ended up being where he wanted to stay rather than hiking or playing frisbee or doing some other random athletic thing that would get his heart rate up where he didn't want it to be anymore. There would be embarrassment then, when he was breathing heavy and squatting like the old man that he was, staring at his too pale legs and rolled over socks. "What are you doing, babe?"

"I...," Jim started, but didn't know how to finish, so he didn't. Instead he turned back to look at the house, to look into the hazy windows, at the shadows on the ceiling.

"Jim..." Brendan said, taking long strides toward him, covering the ground between them quickly.

Jim could feel Brendan's eyes on the side of his face, felt

how hotly they bored into him. He couldn't turn to face him; he didn't want to. There would be frustration in those eyes, maybe even confusion, but those weren't the things that would bother Jim long after they'd left that sidewalk in front of the creepy old house. It would be the hint of disdain in them, hidden behind his beautiful hazel irises, that unnatural glint that would show as if it had been caught in the noonday light. That's what would poke at Jim, nag at him, eat away at him in the middle of the night.

"It's nothing," Jim said, letting his eyes linger on the house a beat longer before turning and smiling at Brendan, looking at him but not looking, not closely at least... giving himself time to recover the way he knew he had to if they were going to move on, have the fun they had intended to when they started out of the house that day. Antiquing Brendan had called it, but Jim recognized it for what it was immediately: shopping. They'd find themselves in an overly expensive shop in some old West Virginia town turned tourist trap by the historic railroad that cut through the hills. They'd buy stuff they wouldn't know what to do with when they got it home, and Jim would shake his head when the credit card statement hit his inbox. But the weather was crisp and clear and the sun was catching all the gold highlights in Brendan's hair.

Jim let himself look at Brendan real that time, make eye contact.

Brendan's eyes were concerned but at least the other things Jim had imagined seeing in them had receded if they were ever there at all.

Jim smiled reassuringly.

Brendan patted Jim on the shoulder then rubbed at it a little rougher than Jim would have liked but beggars couldn't be choosers while standing on a sidewalk in the middle of a chilly morning.

A pause.

Quiet.

Too quiet.

Brendan broke the silence as he nudged Jim, urge him to walk away from the house that had seemed to catch him in its web and hold him there.

And Jim let him.

"Come on. The map says there's a gourmet muffin shop at the end of this street."

"Gourmet muffin shop," Jim said amicably, hoping his voice sounded as skeptical as it normally would have. "Sounds like an oxymoron to me."

And off they went the way they would have before because there really wasn't anything keeping them there, no murk to be mired in, no cement on the bottom of his shoes keeping his feet in place, nothing there, nothing to see, nothing in the window, no shadow moving along the ceiling, nothing—

"Hold on," Brendan said in that way he spoke when something unexpected but fabulously intriguing caught his eye. Jim had learned to both love and fear that tone. "The map didn't say *anything* about this."

"About what?"

Jim looked around for the shiny thing that had caught Brendan's eye but could see nothing but a single level self-storage eyesore that was completely out of place in that little idyllic town, and a cemetery.

No.

"What do you mean 'what'? Do you not see that amazingness in front of you?"

Jim had to fight the urge to cringe at the word choice. There were a lot of things that were amazing in the world: seeing a parrotfish on a dive; sitting on the Lincoln steps at night; the first bite of a warm chocolate croissant among them, but a cemetery? No, not amazing... not in Jim's book.

But Brendan had always loved cemeteries.

"Can you imagine the history?" Brendan said, already walking ahead of Jim toward the open gate. It didn't matter that he had walked ahead—Jim didn't even need to hear him. He could have recited the lines himself. He had already spent countless hours peering at the gravestones of people he didn't know, that no one who was related to him had likely ever known, because Brendan could *feel* the history, was enthralled by the stories of the people who lay beneath their feet. Somewhere along the line Brendan had started looking for the oldest birth year—he had to beat 1754 now—and they had spent what felt like a thousand weekends trying to find it. Time he could never get back. He was not in the mood to do it again, not then, so close to that house with its chipped paint and buckling paneling... paneling that looked like it might be expanding and contracting, as if the house were taking slow, lazy breaths.

"Brendan..." Jim heard himself saying as some part of him wrangled itself out of that weird hazy space he had been in. Brendan was far ahead of him now, almost to the entryway of the cemetery, its weathered stone pillars standing just a little taller than he did at 6'2". If there had been a gate blocking entry before, it was gone now and what would have been the point? The walls that bordered the furthest-most headstones were shorter than waist height. Even if there had been a gate, that wouldn't have stopped Brendan, Jim knew. The lure of "history" would have been too much to ignore and over the wall he would have gone with Jim soon to follow. Keeping him young, Jim rationalized, but that argument left him cold at that moment.

"Bren? Come on, this isn't what we came out here for—" Jim started as he stepped off the sidewalk heading toward the cemetery. He thought he had finished what he intended to say, had maybe added a little bit of an indignant flair at the end to see how that would play, but when he found himself on his ass in the middle of the street looking at a mature tortoiseshell cat with bright green eyes, he knew better. It stood near his feet looking accusatorily at him over its shoulder and Jim instantly knew he had stepped on it, might have even hurt it.

"Hey," he said, his voice taking on a consoling tone he seldom used, "are you ok, buddy?"

Jim leaned toward the cat, marveling at how still it was standing, how beautiful its coat was, how it never hissed at him. He had almost touched it before memories of seeing cats dig their claws into people, climb up their bodies, and find a soft spot to bite stilled his hand in mid-air.

"You're not gonna hurt me, are you buddy? I didn't mean to hurt you."

Jim didn't move his hand.

The cat stayed where it was, fixing him with those gorgeous green eyes.

Jim had time to think that the cat's eyes should be added to the list of amazing things in the world before he felt Brendan drop to his knees beside him.

"Jim! What happened? Are you all right?"

Brendan's hands and eyes were everywhere at once.

"I'm ok, I'm ok," Jim tried but Brendan still checked for blood, checked the ground for something that could have tripped him, checked for anything and everything. "It was just this silly cat. It ran right out in front of me."

Jim turned back to the cat with laughter on his lips that died when he found the space by his foot empty.

"What cat?" Brendan asked.

Jim looked past his toes in the direction the cat might

have run but didn't see any place it could have ducked out of view as quickly as it had.

"There was… it was right there."

Jim disliked how uncertain he sounded but could do nothing to change it.

"It probably just ran off. Had enough excitement for the day," Brendan said as he stood up. He reached down to help Jim, but he wouldn't let him… just couldn't.

"Yeah…" Jim mumbled as he stood, eyes still scanning for the cat, trying to avoid getting a good look at the house with the hazy glass and the shadows on the ceiling as he did.

"Or maybe it's a ghost cat," Brendan said, trying to coax Jim out of whatever was setting him on edge.

Jim responded belatedly. "Y—yeah. A ghost cat. Would make sense around here."

"What?"

The chuckle in Brendan's voice wasn't derisive but something inside Jim wanted to take it that way. It took everything he had not to scowl at the smiling face facing him.

Brendan's eyes searched Jim's face as he spoke words that were code for something else, words that tried to mask the real concern brewing behind them but fell short.

"I was kidding," Brendan said flatly, holding onto the smile even though there was nothing incredulous or even remotely funny about what could be going on in front of him… the thing his family had warned him about when they realized he was serious about Jim… the thing that had already started to haunt his dreams.

Jim blinked and then looked away from Brendan, his eyes searching for the cat even though he knew it was futile. But there was something there. At the edge of his line of sight where things distorted and blurred, merged together, there was *something*.

By the house.

Brendan issued a sound that was meant to be endearing, maybe a bit indulgent as well, but didn't quite work.

"I can think of a hundred other ways you could have told me you didn't want to go into that cemetery," Brendan joked as he smoothed Jim's clothes, fussing over him unconsciously.

"No, it's not that," Jim said without thinking and he immediately wanted to kick himself. Because no, he didn't want to go into the cemetery and look at headstones, stare at the graves of people he didn't know... not again... not ever again if he could help it. But that was less important than the weird tint the world was taking as they stood there on a street they didn't know, in a town they had never been to before. It was like a veil over a camera lens.

"Really, babe, you didn't see it?"

"No," Brendan deadpanned even as a new smile crept onto his face, one designed to lighten the mood, to lighten *Jim*, "I did not see your ghost cat, and I doubt you did either, though this is a bit elaborate to get me to change course."

Jim struggled to keep his expression even, or at least the way it was.

Brendan paused. It told Jim everything he needed to know.

"You really don't like doing these things with me, do you?"

There it was. Jim had two choices: fix it or ruin a perfectly good day.

"Of course I do," he started, but knew he had to change tack to make it stick. "Well, I mean, you know I could never go inside another cemetery and that would be fine by me, but I love doing things with you. You're so... I don't know..."

Brendan's eyes were on him.

"So interested in things. It's refreshing. I love that you let me tag along on your adventures."

Jim hugged Brendan, gave him a real one—none of that hand shaking, shoulder bumping bullshit they usually did outside of the house. He needed to drive the point home, make Brendan see that he was sincere. A bro hug wouldn't cut it.

"So, come on. Let's go in and see if we can beat our year."

Brendan's eyes smiled first and that was good. Jim let him lead the way through the entryway, trying not to let himself see it as an open mouth waiting to swallow them whole. He listened as Brendan first asked Jim if he remembered what the year to beat was then recalled it himself. He nodded and "mm hmmed" when Brendan talked about how much information used to go on tombstones—some of them were as lengthy as obituaries—and how beautiful that was and how everything seemed to be about cold efficiency these days. Jim smiled after Brendan as he moved briskly between tombstones always careful not to step where he thought their bodies were because that, to him, was disrespectful. Jim looked at the stones too, playing along, pulling up the rear as Brendan moved ahead among the weathered, discolored tombstones. Jim had to squint at some of them, the writing worn away. And that was ok. It gave him something to do while Brendan was on his mission. He was used to being left to his own devices in cemeteries: it was par for the course. Brendan was the resident historian in his family. He researched his family's genealogy, figured out that they had been free in America long before the end of slavery, and was still actively trying to trace his lineage back to Africa. He found his Caucasian family first because there were clear records for them. In doing so, he became intrigued by the history that lived on that side of his bloodline—founding father, Native American, change the trajectory of the country type of history. And he was hooked. Jim understood that. He was just thankful Brendan didn't have any charcoal or rice paper in his pockets to rub tombstones.

Jim found the emotions he was supposed to respond with when Brendan talked about the grave with the lamb and the ones that had rocks sitting on top of them. He heard Brendan when he wondered out loud about what was in the over-grown patch, might have grunted a response when Brendan guessed at the birth years of the people to whom the stones buried in the brush belonged, but Jim wasn't entirely sure if he had... not after what he saw. What Brendan would remember about that moment, what he would never speak about but would stay in his head for the rest of his life, was how limp Jim's body had looked as he stood in front of that grave, leaned in close, standing on what Brendan assumed was the deceased's chest. And he never did that, never tram-pled the bodies that way; he maintained the invisible coffin-shaped boundary if for no other reason than breaking it always gave Brendan the willies. That was one of the things that Brendan appreciated about Jim—he would just go along with all of Brendan's hairbrained ideas. So when he turned away from the overgrown spot at the back corner of the cemetery having chickened out of going in because of the possums, rats, and zombies he was suddenly convinced were in there, Brendan was surprised to see Jim standing so close to the headstone, standing over the dead person like a night hag.

Brendan wanted to call out to him but something stopped him. Something told him it was too late, that he would never hear him... that Jim would never be able to hear him again. His mouth felt dry, as though it had been hanging open for a long time, and he supposed, in retrospect, it had.

Jim had first been drawn to the tombstone because it was tall, so tall he could almost read the name without lowering his eyes, and for him, at just under 6 feet tall, that was unusual. But the curiosity he felt about that was usurped quickly enough, rendered unimportant and totally forgotten within the span of a second because the name...

Jim would have told Brendan about the weeping willow above the name, how deep set it was... how purposeful. He would have spoken of the way the name looked as if it had been stamped but the rest of the words were done in a cursive that could have easily been etched into the stone by someone's careful hand. His mother's careful hand. She'd had beautiful handwriting, her loops graceful and sure. She had tried to teach Jim how to write in cursive before he went to school and then again when his teacher's lessons failed but Jim had never quite mastered her artful control. That he hadn't been allowed to write with a pen in school until the 4th grade and not until he was 12 years old at home was something they joked about. He heard her laughter in his ears as he looked upon the stone bearing his name, the one that only his family called him, the one he wished he had heard out loud just one more time. His mother used to sing his name to him, made a song up about him the way she did so many things. She could hardly cook a meal without singing a song of her own creation. There were precious few that she could repeat, as random as her lyrics were, but the one about him was a constant. More poem than song, the melody changed often but not the words.

> *"Jameson Reeves*
> *Born in times of peace*
> *in the year 1961.*
> *Been lots of fun*
> *since his life begun*
> *And will be so until he's done."*

Jim would have told Brendan he wasn't done yet, that he

had more to do, more places to go, more things to see, more graves to visit if that's what he wanted. Jim would have asked him what day it was because didn't they have that thing in the city to go to if it was the Saturday he was thinking it was? Didn't they need to head back home and get ready for it? He would have remarked at how creepy it was to see Jim's name and birthday on such an old headstone and Brendan would have wanted to take a picture of it—a picture he would never look at because it was, indeed, extremely creepy to see his uncommon name with his exact birthday on a tombstone that looked centuries old. And the other part... well, that just couldn't be right, not if he had the right Saturday in mind and they had that event in the city that night. Jim would have shown Brendan that curious date, asked him if he ever heard of someone memorializing such a bad joke. They'd seen a few doozies together—it was as if, at some point in time, people went out of their way to write unique epitaphs. He remembered the tombstone that read "Shit Happens" and Porky Pig's famous sign off. They had found one that talked about someone owing another person money on their last outing. But had someone ever carved a future date of death into a tombstone? Were they even allowed to do that? Wouldn't somebody be afraid that some bastard might try to make it come true?

A splash of color caught his eye. Sunflowers on the ground, the golden yellow stark against the paling green grass. Jim's favorite.

Jim opened his mouth to tell Brendan about the tombstone with its weird date, today's date if he had the right Saturday in mind, about how weird it was to be seeing it there under the name he apparently shared with this poor sap whose family or friends or somebody thought it would be a great gag to pay for a headstone with a future death date on it, to mention how beautiful—yes, amazing—the sunflowers were, but he couldn't find his voice. The sun was different now; its heat no longer muted by the cool air that had tousled Jim's hair as they walked, as he stood looking at the house with its shadows on the ceiling. Jim could see the sun, how bright it was, but its warmth didn't make it to his skin and he wanted to comment about that to the man standing before him, wanted to move out of the way of the grave he had come to visit, the grave he had thrown the sunflowers onto

onto his chest. The flowers are on his chest

and let him visit in peace, but not before that bit of small talk, that affirmation that he felt the lack of heat too. But as he looked into the man's watery, eyes, the greenish brown irises going hazy with cataracts, as the sunlight seemed to get smothered by his dull gray hair, Jim realized he already knew.

NIGHT VISION

IF YOU WATCH the road at night, when the world's asleep and
the air is still, you can see them. A bubble, nothing more than
a flex, so slight you don't know if you really saw it. Subtle,
like a corpse exhaling. Summer heat shifts the asphalt to
crack, to open, to let, and they come in droves under the light
of the moon. Iridescent translucence with a red-hot core, like
blood coursing through veins in a clear husk as they survey
the terrain. Plotting, scheming, planning, they move through
manmade boundaries as if they weren't there. They stand at
the foot of the bed, hide in the webbing of dust in the
corners, measuring effort, sizing us up. They smile when
they see us, like lights shining through windows and
reflecting on the wall.

If you watch the road at night you'll see them when they
retreat, their bellies full of dead skin and hair, nail clippings
and earwax, satiated by the taste, the touch, the smell. You'll
see them hesitate, unsure if they should leave or stay,
conquer or acquiesce... again. Don't let them see you hiding
as they dip beneath the surface. Don't let them sense your

fear because they are waiting, always waiting for the right moment, the right reason—any reason—to stay.

WHAT NATURE KEEPS

TREES SWAY IN THE WIND, their leaves moving like wet hair shaken joyfully, clean and fresh. They whisper secrets to each other; the wind carries the tales from one to the other down the line, threading through the wood like fingers combing, massaging, adoring. Leaves undulate, take flight like children clasping hands, making airplane wings to fly, fly fly. They steal the moments to enrich the soil, to feed the bark, and nurture the beasts that call it home. *Don't tell them*, they whisper as the branches reach out to prick skin, draw blood... to feed, *never let them see.*

THE MAKING OF A LOVE STORY

Monday, April 24

6:44 AM I taste your skin in my dreams.
I can feel the curves of your chest and arms against my own

6:46 AM sry. Up early

7:02 AM u up?

7:35 AM yt?

8:11 AM Thinking...

. . .

8:37 AM Take me

8:53 AM Take me

9:28 AM Take me

? 9:28 AM

9:29 AM 'Take me,' I whispered as your tongue searched
for my treasures and caressed them.

9:30 AM I sat quietly in the moonlight that streak
your hair
with majestic silver.
'Touch me', my heart begged but you laughed
low and sultry.

9:32 AM I blushed under the navy sky.

Wym 10:05 AM
the fuck? 10:09 AM
when dis?

10:09 AM I beg you
Touch me.
With your strong hands, hold me.

Yo… 11:10 AM
I can't come thru til l8r

11:10 AM Hum lightly the melody of the
twilight dance so I might meet you
among the stars.

… 11:11 AM
mkay 11:15 AM

11:15 AM Call me stupid
call me dumb
call me anything

No diss r u ok? 11:37 AM

11:38 AM Feeling insane

Word 11:39 AM
yeah, got that gud gud

11:39 AM Possession and jealousy
all in the game

tmi rn fr fr 11:40 AM

11:40 AM You are the only one alive
who can make me feel inside
that I want to be your bride

. . .

W tf 11:41 AM

11:45 AM Screaming silence that shatters eardrums

11: 48 AM Kill me softly as sweet sounds escape my lips

11:51 AM yt?

11:57 AM yt??

12:02 PM rly?

12:05 PM u gud?

12:06 PM sry

12:07 PM jk

12:08 PM fr jk

12:10 PM srsly

12:11 PM ok ttyl jk ok?

12:12 PM k?

1:10 PM yt?

1: 11 PM we gud?

2:05 PM ily
Jk

2:10 PM jk fr

. . .

2:25 PM xxxxxxx

3:28 PM srsly

3:48 PM omfg

4:06 PM sos

4:07 PM wtf

4:58 PM cul
k?

5:41 PM fr?

8:11 PM come thru soon?

8:12 PM babe?

8:15 PM babe??

8:59 PM …

10:31 PM The rustling of the leaves
The warmth of a breeze
They bring me to my knees since...

10:33 PM My pleasure has dissipated.
Life seems so complicated.

10:34 PM No sensation has penetrated since...

10:35 PM I feel your skin in my hands.

10:36 PM I shut my eyes and trace your face

10:37 PM hoping to keep its contours fixed in my mind

10:39 PM Ooh, to feel your warmth

10:40 PM Your skin, so close, almost my own
Warming

10:41 PM sheltering
consuming
my being

10:46 PM Against me, stay
protect me always

10:47 PM warm me ever

THE DEAD MAN'S COUCH

WILLIE HEARD the older folks talking about it; his parents and the neighbors had used hushed tones to gossip about what happened as they watched the family pull into the driveway, go into the house, and begin the process of dismantling a man's life. They asked each other if the other had ever seen those people before—this *family* that caravanned from parts unknown with a moving truck in tow, ready to take what they wanted from the man's life and discard the rest. They spoke with anger in their voices... anger and disgust... and something else too. Something sharp that he couldn't identify because it was buried beneath emotions that his nine-year-old mind *could* figure out, and those were more than enough. His mother shook her head and the neighbor who fed all the stray cats, cats that left surprises on everyone's lawn and yowled late at night, sighed because 'He' was dead. Had died somewhere in the house.

Alone.

Willie listened as they talked about 'Him', about how meticulous he was about his lawn, about how he painted his mailbox stand every year, about how no one ever saw him at the store or in town, like he didn't exist outside of his driveway. They guessed at how long he had lived there, houses away for some but in Willie's and his parent's cases, right next door. Ten years? Fifteen? To Willie, he had always been there, had always been part of the fabric of the neighborhood, as much backdrop as the street signs and the houses themselves were. But no one seemed to know his name. Willie didn't, and he was sure none of his friends did either. He thought for sure his mother would, living next to him for however long she had, but she wasn't saying it. He knew from experience that when his mother knew someone's name she would use it, would say it more than she needed to, almost as if she were trying to remember it. But she wasn't doing that then as she spoke with Ms. Lenore from three doors down. No one was.

That bothered Willie.

He didn't say much, the man who he'd lived next to all of his life. He never said much of anything to the kids who cut through his yard en route to the bus stop, nor to the people who let their dogs urinate on his lawn. He was invisible unless you looked hard enough and caught the brim of the sun hat that was as much a part of his persona as everything else was. He was always just *there* but not anymore. Now he was gone.

Dead.

Alone in his house.

The man's family was making short work of clearing out the space. They had brought out dressers and boxes full of whatever old men kept in their closets, tucked in the back in the dark. They had brought out a dining room table that looked like it had never been used and a bike that most surely hadn't been ridden in decades. All those things sat in the driveway waiting to be put into the truck and taken back to wherever his "family" came from to be divvyed up and sold, showcased, whatever. Maybe they'd tell a story about who had owned it first, but maybe not. Willie would never know. He figured he shouldn't care, thought that was an odd thing to think about anyway, but still, he did.

They were bringing out a couch now. Two guys who looked like they were old, but not as old as his mother... definitely not as old as 'The Man' who had lived there with his perfectly trimmed bushes and emerald green grass, carried it out grunting and groaning every step of the way. Their foreheads glistened with sweat. One of them cursed when they put it down on the driveway in line behind the other things waiting to be hoisted into the moving truck, hissing something about catching his finger between the asphalt and the wooden base. He shook his hand and cursed again before noticing that Willie was watching him. He jammed his finger into his mouth and softened his eyes, smiled around the digit, which had started to bleed, and waved hello with his uninjured hand. Willie smiled back, let him believe that it was all good, that his Jedi mind trick designed to disarm the nosy kid had worked. The man went inside, finger still in his mouth, a curse still on his lips. Willie watched him go back into the house, wondering what else he might drag out with him the next time he emerged, but as soon as the door slammed shut, his eyes shifted back to the couch. It was white, but not really—more like a grayish pearl. It had a striped pattern: bluish purple flowers in the middle of two thin lines of the same color blue repeated on the surface opposite a swath of solid gray/pearl with some kind of embroidery in the sick-looking solid. The arms had metal balls that looked like studs running up from the base to spiral in the center. And it was worn. The cushions were weathered and stained in some places. It was old timey but not in an antique kind of way—more like it had been in that house since the 1980s, had worn a groove into the rug all its own.

Willie knew it would have stayed there forever if those guys hadn't yanked it out of its cave.

He looked back at the house to see if anyone was coming and saw no one. There wasn't anybody out on the street either, not walking or driving, which was odd for that time of day but Willie didn't think about that. It was just him and the couch. Alone.

Willie cleared the few steps between himself and the couch tentatively, curious but apprehensive. His hand led the way, reaching toward the sickly gray upholstery with a finger that was both eager to touch the couch and afraid to, but before he knew it, without even feeling himself move toward it, sink into it, lay the bare flesh of his thigh where his shorts rode up to revel pale skin against it, Willie was sitting on it, his weight depressing the cushions. A faint, stale smell of cologne wafted up to his nose, encircled his head, made him dizzy. It was hot. The heat from his body was making the cushions warm, so warm that his leg began to sweat, that *he* began to sweat and wet the couch, to *soak* the thing, there was so much. His palms lay flat on the cushion next to his sides, his skin tingling against it, alive with electricity, but that did not scare him... neither did the sound of voices around him, disembodied and rapid-fire, shouting things at him, spitting them, beseeching him the way his 5th grade teacher had the year before when she asked the class to focus because the topic she was covering was important, so very important. One of those voices was his mother's and even though she sounded strange, he could tell it was her. Even through the distortion that kept her voice from his ears, like she was under the water that lay beneath the fog at the other end of a tunnel, Willie could still make out her meaning. Any kid would, if they'd been a kid like him, one who forgot to check in from time to time and came in ten minutes after he was supposed to on hot summer nights. She wanted him to—

Willie smiled when 'He' laughed, wondering if he had always sounded like that... like he had tossed a handful of rocks into his mouth and gargled them with what... water? His own blood? Willie didn't know. He didn't ask 'The Man', who sat next to him on the couch in his driveway, posted up on the rotting thing in the broad daylight, rays of light shooting through him like the sun does a cloud on an otherwise beautiful day, what happened. He didn't ask because he could keep a secret too.

THROUGH THE LOOKING GLASS

AIR.

She needed air and even the stale bathroom in the back of the two-room funeral home would do.

There were still a few minutes before the service would start, and she intended to use all of them there in that tiny little space. Besides, they'd wait for her, wouldn't they? Even though she wasn't the belle of the ball, she *was* paying for this shindig after all. It would be in poor taste to start the service when the wife of the deceased was holed up in the bathroom.

Emma looked at herself in the mirror, going through the motions to keep up the ruse. She was freshening up, tending to the smeared mascara and the makeup withering under the weight of the day. But that's not why she was in there, not really. She hated things like this. Funerals. All the crying. All the 'I'm sorrys' and the platitudes that dripped from people's lips as they streamed by. Hated it. She would have rather had Dominic cremated and taken his ashes out to the woods to spread. But no. No one else wanted that, not his siblings, not his children, not their friends. No one but her. So here she was.

Emma sighed as she looked at herself, at the 'she' that she was now, post-Dominic. Post her end of college hook-up-turned-boyfriend-turned-husband. Post her friend-turned-lover. She looked at herself, at the hair that looked different than it had the morning Dominic died because she was at the hair salon when he died at his desk, was under the dryer when the EMTs tried but failed to revive him. Did he recognize her with the short hair? Emma hadn't mentioned what she was going to do, thought she'd surprise him with it, but he never got to see. Was he looking for her now, looking for an anchor and finding someone who looked like her but with short red hair that he didn't recognize?

Emma looked at herself, searching her eyes for the woman who showed up when she was feeling vulnerable, the girl she had once been before the years had passed and age had added weight and bitterness to her carefree frame... the girl she was beneath the years. And she was there, right there, staring back with a smirk on her face. The sun was kissing her skin, highlighting her hair with gold. And she beckoned older Emma to look closer, to go to her, to become her again. Emma could see the street where she stood, knew that the movie theater stood opposite her, just out of view, and that her favorite bookstore stood next to it and had a cat winding through the display in the window. She knew that younger Emma was going into the bookstore, and she wanted to go with her. The movie would come later, when she and her friends would go out on the town, such as it was. Home from college but living in a two-light village: the movies and dinner was as good as it got. Emma would see more friends from high school there, friends who didn't know what she did when she was away at school, didn't know about the boys she'd met and the things she'd done. They'd do their own things too when they separated again after a few days, when break was over and it was time to get back to the books, and she wouldn't know what they did either. But none of that mattered because they knew each other better than any of those college friends could. The insecurities, the good, the bad, and no one could take that from them... not then or ever.

Max was there.

He wouldn't be on the Harley that he'd die on in 15 years, but he'd be there. And Emma wanted to go there too, to that street at that moment when the cat's tail threatened to knock over John Saul's precariously perched new release. She wanted to go there and hug him and never let go. She didn't love him anymore, hadn't for years before he would meet his end on a lonely road between Winchester and Roanoke, but Emma wanted to hold him there, keep him safe, keep him alive. On that day, when the cat treated the books like dominos and the sun would set with one of the most beautiful displays of color she would ever see, Max was alive and happy. He hadn't started working at the radio station yet, hadn't realized his "On Air" voice yet. Emma hadn't taken Russian Lit yet and wouldn't have met Dominic on the quad after running back to class to pick up the companion book she'd need, the one that took her forever to find in the first place... the one she would fail without. She wouldn't have met Dominic yet and maybe she never would, not if Emma hugged Max tight, tight enough to make him remember how much he liked it when she did that. Maybe they would have gotten back together, bought a little house, had a few kids. Maybe Max wouldn't be dead.

Maybe Dominic wouldn't either.

Max smiled at her from that place way back when and Emma cried in response because he was dead, he was dead, and so was Dominic, the love of her life, the man she had planned to grow old with. And now she was old and he was gone.

Emma sucked her teeth at the young version of her who had started waving at her to get her attention, to make her look closer and climb in. She sucked her teeth and adjusted the wayward red strands that danced along her forehead. She swiped at her eyes and blotted the mascara she had foolishly put on before taking the deep breath that wiped young Emma and Max out of existence for now... maybe even forever. She didn't have time for them, not anymore.

She had a funeral to attend.

SPOILED

I DIDN'T ASK for this, the cold disinterest, the impassive grunts of response and affirmation, sentiment unheard.

I didn't ask for this, the pregnant pauses and pus-filled boils bursting on blemished skin that burnished scars of red with high sheen.

I didn't ask for this but he did, and he always gets what he wants, especially when he screams.

NO REST

"ANYWAY, they dared him to stay there overnight, so he went to the cemetery and sat by one of those big tombstones—the wide ones that look like they're for two graves or something. He sat with his back against it and read the name engraved in the weathered stone out loud. 'Matilda Carter' it said, and when he read her date of death, he realized it was that same date!"

Amanda paused for effect, and Tim and Anna started laughing, the sound bursting from them as if breaking through a taped-up box. Ray didn't want to laugh, was trying his best not to even crack a smile at the girl he was planning to ask to marry him in a few months, the one he had bought a ring for already and building up the nerve to give her, but he did. It was just so cheesy, so predictable that he couldn't help it. He didn't know what he was expecting from her or any of them, really—none of them did. This was the first time they had decided to tell stories at a cemetery at night; it was their first time hanging out at a cemetery at all, regardless of the time, so it wasn't like any of them knew the etiquette. But, Amanda drew the short stick, so she set the bar. Ray would have to try hard not to blow it out of the water.

"What?" Amanda said indignantly. He knew that sound, understood what it meant. He forced his laughter to die in his throat.

"It's just so obvious," Anna said, flicking hair dismissively. "It's not scary when there's no, I don't know, *soul*."

Anna was pontificating again, talking like she knew everything about everything, like she was so enlightened about the world. Amanda hated when Anna got like that, acting like just because she would be going off to an Ivy League school after summer was over and Amanda was heading to the community college a mile away she was somehow better than her. Amanda looked like she might push Anna if she kept talking like that, like she definitely would bang her head on one of those headstones 'by mistake'—just enough to make her feel it—if she didn't shut up.

"Yeah, and how could he read the name on the tombstone if his back was against it? He wouldn't be able to see it. And don't say it's the tombstone in front of him because they don't put names on the back of tombstones," Tim said, and true or not, Ray didn't like the way he sounded. He was siding with Anna just because that's what he always did— everything Anna ever said was magically so amazing and accurate and totally profound and no one else could say or do or think anything better. Tim was being condescending and he was pandering to a girl who still didn't give him the time of day. But he still thought he had a shot and because of that, Tim talked like she did —you could see up his nostrils as high as he tilted his head most of the time just so he could look down his nose at people. Or at least he and Amanda. Ray didn't like the way the conversation was changing, turning into something serious, something mean, a challenge that went unstated but was as much an 'us versus them' as it could be. He didn't like it one bit.

"Do you have a better one?" Ray asked, cutting Amanda off right when she started talking. By the look on her face, he had saved Tim... he had saved them all. "You're busy laughing but I don't hear you scaring anybody."

"Yet," Tim added and straightened up to start telling his story.

Tim began, talking in a hushed tone that was as uncertain as it was pretentious, especially once he realized that everyone was looking at him, including Anna, and that it was otherwise quiet in the cemetery. It was dark, and the place was closed, so of course it was quiet, but there was something about the cemetery in the dark that didn't sit right with Ray—wouldn't sit right with anyone if they had half a mind.

Ray looked at Tim whose eyes had grown wide in response to the chill in the air, the darkened sky, the realization that they really were out there in the middle of the night. He kept talking but his eyes said something different than his mouth did.

Fuck, what were they doing there?

"Not yet, chile, not yet!"

They heard the voice at the same time. Tim's words stopped, cut off like a switch, the echo waving in the air for the shortest of seconds after it was gone. They whipped their heads in the direction of the sound, all the while telling themselves that it was nothing, a bird, a wolf, damn it, but nothing else, not what they were afraid of, not what their nightmares were made of.

They saw her. She was three rows over and she was lurching, her gait interrupted by whatever she was pulling along behind herself. It was slowing her down, was awkward and making her stumble but she was determined to bring it along anyway. They crouched behind the tombstone they were in front of, trying to make themselves small, willing themselves not to run to their car. But she didn't look in their direction; her eyes remained trained on the grave she was heading towards. When she got to it, she threw the sack on the ground in front of it and slapped the marble face with an open hand.

"There you go, you bitch, there you go," she said, her voice slurring though they didn't see a bottle. "Drink up."

The woman was clad in a business suit and heels. Her pantyhose had a run in them, noticeably beyond the salvation of clear nail polish. Her hair was in a not-so-neat bun. Her makeup was streaked, her mouth painted a too—dark plum.

They couldn't tear their eyes away from her.

"Make it last," she growled, her voice thick with emotion. She kicked the tombstone, the heel of her shoe breaking against it, almost falling backward from the force, "'cuz I'm not ready yet."

Anna gasped as the woman plucked off one nail and then another, taking them off at the cuticle, ripping them from the nailbed like they were press-ons but they weren't, they weren't, because the blood spurted up from them, up like a fountain, like one of those stone frogs spitting on flowers in a garden. Anna gasped, and it was so loud, so obnoxious, so utterly damning, and the woman looked.

She looked right at them.

Ray wondered if Anna knew what she had done, if she realized that she had bought the woman the extra time she wanted—four times more than the thing in the sack would have gotten her. He wondered if Tim knew what his ignorant crush had done with her college-bound, smart-aleck mouth. He wondered if Amanda would push Anna out front before Ray could do it himself.

THE PITCH

"Ok, so imagine you're sitting on the train taking selfies or maybe doing a live or something like that and then someone starts acting crazy. At first it looks like a prank, just some dumb shit—oh, sorry—but you know, the same stupid stuff you see on the train every day, but then they start, like, killing people," the guy said animatedly, his hands bracketing the space in front of him as if he was holding a box that was jiggling around of its own volition. He was in his mid-40s, judging by the wrinkles popping up on his forehead, but trying not to look like it; his clothes screamed 20-something, but not just any 20-something... a 20-something who was a fashion influencer, finger on the pulse of pop culture but in a casual way type of guy. He was selling his idea hard; his eyes almost bugged out of his head with excitement. It made Julie tired.

"Think *28 Days* meets a New York City subway station, right? Totally enclosed—there's no way out."

"Running zombies," Julie supplied.

"Running zombies, yes!" He banged the table. "See, you get exactly what I'm saying, right? And they're falling down the stairs, falling onto the tracks, getting crushed by the train coming into the station. The girl—well, *I* see it as a girl, but it can be whatever you want it to be, right?—she's doing her Live and—"

He started gesticulating wildly. Julie didn't know if she was excited for or afraid of the jazz hands that were likely to start up soon.

"—she catches all of this in her video but she doesn't notice—she's too busy looking at herself, right? So the people watching are like, 'Girl! Watch out!' and she doesn't know what they mean and she's all smiling for the camera and her followers or whatever and then, you know…"

Julie waited, holding her tongue. She'd have to leave him in a moment, she knew that, but for a few seconds more, she wanted to wait to see what he would say.

Five seconds.

Ten.

Twenty.

Uncomfortable now.

Twenty-five.

"What?" Julie asked, knowing the answer, but hoping against hope that there was more to it than there seemed.

He squirmed in his seat. His hands drew in, more of a parenthesis than a bracket.

"You know… she dies. They all… die."

Even he knew that wasn't enough.

"The zombies get them?" Julie asked, just to be sure he understood that she understood that there was nothing else to the story.

"Yeah," he started, searching for something else to add but finding nothing. "The zombies get them, but maybe not all of them."

Epiphany!

"Maybe they only get some of them and the others fight them off."

"And then what?" Julie prompted, knowing what would be next so well she could recite it with him.

"Well, then they would escape the subway and keep going, keep running, right? Head for the suburbs where there are less people —"

"Like every other zombie movie," Julie finished, putting him out of his misery. He didn't stop talking, but she had stopped listening. She thought about turning her camera off to see if he would get the point, but decided she wasn't that person... not yet.

" —and it could be whatever you want, you know? You could go survivor view or zombie view. Yeah! It could be a whole different kind of party then, right? There's so much you could do —"

" —with an old horror antagonist that owes its resurgence to a comic book."

He looked at her in confusion.

It took everything she had not to snort.

"Thanks so much for telling me about your idea. I will give it some thought."

"Yeah, cool. And remember, right, it can be whatever you guys want to do. I'm totally flexible, right? I mean, you guys know best, and—"

"Thanks, sure," she cut in, looking at her wrist at the nonexistent watch telling her she was late for her nightly series binge.

"Right? And it would be super cool if—"

"Ok, yeah, goodnight."

She left the meeting.

She left the meeting while he was mid-sentence.

She left the meeting after talking over him and he was mid-sentence.

Damn.

She was turning into a bitch.

But he wasn't going to stop, she told herself as she prepared for her next round. He was going to keep going even though he knew the idea sounded like everything else— maybe a different setting, but maybe not; Julie thought she might have seen a zombie apocalypse in a subway done before, maybe before streaming, maybe even coming out of another country. He was never going to stop, even though he knew it was a lost cause so she had to save herself. Maybe she could have done it differently. Ok, she'd admit that much, but in the end what was done was done.

She opened a new video call. The woman waiting for her was visibly nervous. The lighting didn't do anything to help the situation at all—it threw blue on their shared screen making her skin appear almost translucent. This made Julie feel like she could see the woman's veins, the one in the center of her forehead specifically. And that vein was pulsating.

"Ok…" Julie paused to confirm the name, causing the woman to shift in her seat.

"… Val. Whatcha got for me today?"

Val took a deep breath and then began.

"Singer in a band that was popular like 20 years ago meets his current wife, the one who is ready to leave him now, at a signing after a show… only the show was way back when— like way back before the band even had a deal."

Julie nodded.

Val nodded, eyes widened and chin dipped conspiratorially.

Julie waited.

Waited some more.

"Go on," Julie said, more than a little anxious to hurry it all up.

"Yeah, so, he wakes up, and the day is normal. He does a show unconsciously looking for this estranged wife in the crowd even though she shouldn't be there—she lives on the other side of the country—but doesn't find her at first but then, when they are about to leave the stage he sees her and she's young. He asks his bandmates if they saw her but," she shakes her head and sits back from the camera, relaxing into the story, "they didn't."

Another pause that Julie dutifully waited through, but this time it didn't seem like Val was going to say anything else. She waited a beat longer before speaking again.

"And...?"

Val looked at Julie like she had spoken in another language. Then she offered,

"The woman... she wasn't there...?"

Julie was talking before she meant to be. Had she had a chance to slow herself down, she might not have added so much edge to her voice.

"What is the big deal about this, Val? It's cool, sure, maybe even a little creepy, but where are you going with it? Is this going to be a life on different planes/alternate reality kind of thing? Is it horror? If so, how? Is it romance? If so, it needs a little edge. What do you want people to get out of it? What will they talk about after the last scene?"

Val looked nervous again, and this time Julie didn't care as much.

"I don't know... I mean, I guess it could be a romance," Val started. "Maybe they find each other again after all that time. Maybe he was tripping or something and he just keeps imagining her."

It was Julie's turn to shake her head this time.

"You haven't written this yet, have you?"

"Well, no, I thought I was here to talk about my —"

"Your *script*. You're here to talk about your script, not

pitch an idea so you can go write a script and then think I'm going to do something with it. You're not there yet."

"But they said —"

"Put some bite into your idea and get it on paper. Come back next year."

Julie left the meeting, this time totally ok with doing so. She looked at the time. Ten minutes until this chore was over. She'd have to take one more person. Julie sighed, closed her eyes. She was irritated that she was there: manning pitch sessions wasn't exactly the highlight of a film festival and online made it even worse. You were truly a captive audience then, each person looking at you, your backdrop, your personal space and assessing it, whether for meaning, relevance to the discussion, or just to be nosy. It was exhausting, but somebody had to do it and she had drawn the short straw that year. The good thing was that she wouldn't have to do it again the next year—she'd get to have drinks or screen a film or just sleep if she wanted to instead. She could do whatever she wanted, which was anything but this.

Ten more minutes.

One more pitch.

She took a deep breath and opened the call.

… And there was silence. Silence and blackness. It seemed like no one was on the call, yet her window had adjusted to accommodate two videos. Whoever was on the other side didn't have their camera turned off or their sound muted. It was just… blank.

"Hello?" Julie said the same way she would answer a call from a phone number she didn't recognize, the lilt of her voice as it rose to form the questions loud in her ear.

Nothing.

There was no silhouette—it wasn't like someone had dialed in from a dark place and didn't have the right lighting to illuminate themselves properly. It was as if the camera were shooting a black wall.

"If you're there, I can't see you. Can you turn your camera on?"

That had been one of the rules. You had to have your camera on to pitch your screenplay. As festivals tried to pivot and figure out how to make the online experience worth the price of admission, several changes had been made to the process. There were online movie screenings and forums for feedback, panel discussions you could watch live and pre-recorded material as well. There would be an awards cere-mony that no one would attend in person. And then there was this virtual pitch thing she had been doing for the last hour. Several houses were doing it, including some indie outfits. The rules stated that both parties had to have their cameras on and have adequate microphones. They also stated that there shouldn't be a whole lot of distractions either—dogs barking and your kid playing his drum kit in the basement were not welcome. It was ten minutes of time —if you couldn't spare that, don't sign up.

Easy peasy. Yet here she sat with a blank screen.

Julie sighed and fingered the edge of a bradded screen-play sitting on the desk. She hadn't planned to read it; it had a pink cardstock cover, for God's sakes, so she had planned to throw it in the trash, but she opened it instead. It would give her something to do while the person on the other end sorted out their problem. She read, smirking expectantly.

INT. POST OFFICE—MR. LEVY'S OFFICE—EVENING
MR. LEVY, a mid —forties, overweight, balding man paces
the floor in his office. He walks to the door and LOOKS at
the empty lobby. He walks back to the mailroom and SEES
Cal smoking a cigarette and talking to POSTAL
WORKER #2.

MR. LEVY
Cal.

Cal looks up.

MR. LEVY
(continuing; sternly)
Come into my office, Cal.

Mr. Levy retreats back into the office.

CAL
(mumbling)
I wonder what the hell he wants now.

POSTAL WORKER #2
Sounds like you're in deep shit.

CAL
He's always bustin' my ass for somethin'.

POSTAL WORKER #2
Same shit, different day.

CAL
Yeah, you ain't kiddin'.

POSTAL WORKER #2
I'll see you later, Cal.

CAL
Yeah.
Cal walks trepidatiously into Mr. Levy's office.

CAL
(continuing)
You wanted to see me?

MR. LEVY
Yes, I did.
Mr. Levy sits down with effort.

CAL
What's this about?

MR. LEVY
It's about your behavior.

Cal looks closely at Mr. Levy.
MR. LEVY

(continuing)
I've been watching the way you handle customers, and I have
to tell you, Cal, I don't like what I see.

*Mr. Levy's sweat is forming a ring around his underarms. Cal is
getting MAD.*
MR. LEVY

(continuing)
Now, I've told you about this kind of thing before, and it
hasn't gotten any better since then. As a matter of fact, it's
gotten worse!

CAL
I don't think I understand what you mean, Mr. Levy.

Julie exhaled incredulously and made a show of depositing the screenplay in the trashcan next to the desk as she mumbled under her breath,

"Going postal... I mean... do people even go to the post office anymore?"

The screen was still blank.

"Hello?" she said, irritated.

She could just hang up and Julie really thought about doing just that because the event was pretty much over anyway and who would care. But then she thought about whether or not they were logging time somehow, could see that she kicked off early. If they could and that bought her another year of manning the pitch booth she'd gnaw at her own wrists.

"Hello? Are you there?"

Nothing.

"Look, you're supposed to have your camera on, so..."

Nothing.

Maybe they had a bad connection? Had gotten kicked out somehow? How long was she expected to stay if no one responded?

The recording light, the inconspicuous little dot, showed itself in the corner of the screen. Yeah, they were watching.

Julie sighed, looked at the clock.

Seven minutes.

Seven minutes, seven minutes. She could do anything for seven minutes.

She tapped her desk, looked around her room. Took out a screenplay they had bought and got back to marking it up.

She waited.

Four minutes.

Julie shook her head after checking the time and went back to work. But then she lifted her head to stare at the screen. What if they thought she should have logged out, should have picked up another call instead of goofing off in the room doing nothing? The festival folks—they really take pride in their programming and if she wasn't pulling her weight, her boss might hear about it.

Julie's eyes flicked over to the recording button. It was still on.

"H —hey... is someone there?" she tried but got no response. She tried clicking around on the screen just in case it had gone to sleep and somehow kept the call visible, even though that didn't make a ton of sense to her. She was grasping at straws.

Julie leaned closer, trying to decipher movement in the other video, so when it happened she was too close to see it for what it was. It was only when she leaned back in her seat, resigned to the fact that she was either going to catch hell for wasting 10 minutes editing a screenplay that was already bought and paid for or slip under the radar that she saw something in the other video screen. It was an outline of her head—black on black, so it was difficult to see , but it was surely there. Julie could see her hairstyle, pulled up in a ponytail, windswept bang over her forehead. She could see her large hoop earring and the absence of one in the other ear. She could see her features, engraved on the black like ink, her teeth an outlined block.

Her eyebrows furrowed.

The action was mirrored onscreen.

She leaned closer and the reflection did the same, some weird doppelganger dance with her computer twin. When she was young, she'd had an idea about something like this happening, but it was in a mirror. She had pulled her medicine cabinet mirror open one day and held it against the big rectangular one in the bathroom she and her sister shared, creating at least 10 reflections—little Julies standing in the mirror wearing a parochial school outfit. She remembered thinking that it would be creepy if somewhere way back in the line of reflections, one of them changed; if that Julie turned her head or changed her expression or something like that. She remembered thinking that would be an excellent movie.

She didn't see the hand come through the screen to caress her face until it was too late: she was too busy staring at her eyes reflected in the pitch, the emptiness and recognition inside battling each other for first dibs. It was the mouth that won, the mouth, dripping with something black and viscous... something she felt roll down her chin—the mouth that made the first cut, and that was the way it should be, after all.

In her head as much as with her ears, Julie heard a voice that sounded like it was speaking from underwater ask the question that had frightened her into a corner before she had jumped the desk, taken ownership of it, and fashioned it into a weapon more times than she cared to admit. That it would be the last thing she would ever hear never dawned on her— she was too busy taking in the shape of her eyes reflected in ink, like a coin stamped with a stencil that was too wide for it —but if it had, she wouldn't have been surprised.

She almost let the hand that came from the screen cradle her head, the hand that wouldn't show up on the recording when staff looked back to try and figure out what happened to Julie Stafford from Media Mix and why she stood up her last appointment. Indeed, the video wouldn't show much of anything—mostly the top of her head as she read something on her desk and the occasional glance at the screen. The tech tasked with reviewing that meeting was about to turn off the feed when he noticed Julie leaning forward, her head cocked to the side in an unnatural way. It gave him the chills—he would never say it that way, but it was the truth. Her chin seemed to reach toward the screen, tilting her head to the side and distending her neck. When she spoke the last word she ever would, he didn't jump—that wasn't the thing that made him call his manager in and tell him to check it out. That she had said, 'And...?' seemingly unprovoked was weird, but what made him stand up and back away from his desk was when she looked at the camera dead on, seemed to look right at him and, with her neck too long and her chin thinned into a point as if someone were squeezing the flesh there, she smiled.

9-1-1

"9-1-1. WHAT'S YOUR EMERGENCY?"

"Oh my god… oh no!"

"Ma'am, tell me what your emergency is."

"There's… there's… I think…"

"Ma'am, I need you to calm down and —"

" —there's a m-man… I think it's Charlie…"

"Do you know the man? What is he doing?"

"It's Charlie… I mean, I *think* it's him. But he-he's been in some kind of accident, I guess. Some kind of—"

"There's been an accident? Did it happen where you are now—579 Sycamore Lane?"

"No, no… I mean yes, that's where we—oh my God!"

"I'm sorry, ma'am. I just need you to tell me what you see. I'm sending help right now, just tell me what is going on."

"He's-he's… Mitchell… he's heading for Mitchell."

"Mitchell?"

"My neighbor. Charlie… he's trying to—"

"Ma'am, please calm down. I assure you, help is on the way."

'Mitchell! Over here! Hurry!'

"Ma'am —"

'No... no! NOOOOO!'

"Ma'am?"

"Oh my God."

"Ma'am?"

"Mitchell..."

"What happened to Mitchell? Is he with you now? Mitchell... he's your neighbor?"

"Oh, dear God."

"Ma'am, wha—."

"His neck... I can't believe what happened to his neck, oh God."

"What happened to *whose* neck, ma'am?"

"...neck, it's..."

"Was he in the accident also? Are you saying there's damage to Mitchell's neck?"

"He... he... he..."

"... ma'am?"

"Charlie..."

"Help is coming for Charlie, ma'am. But is there another injured party? Where is Mitchell?"

"Mitchell is outside. With Charlie. They're both outside."

"Ok, help is on the way. They will take care of Charlie and Mitchell, if he needs help too."

"No. No! Don't let them get close —"

"Ma'am, everything will be ok. You just stay here on the line with me. Help will be there very soon."

"No... they can't help Charlie. He... oh my God... nononono!"

"What's happening ma'am? What's the matter?"

"Mitchell is back. He's back. It's impossible."

"Mitchell from before? Your neighbor?"

"Yes. He's back. He shouldn't be here. Shouldn't be—not after... Charlie... they —."

"It's ok, ma'am. We've got enough room for them both in the rig. They'll get the help they need. Do you know what hap —"

"*He* did it. Charlie... he—they're trying to get in."

"Try to keep them still until the ambulance comes. They shouldn't be moving around too mu—"

'*Get away! Get away, you son of a bitch! Noooooooo!*'

"Ma'am?"

'*...Na... no...*'

"Ma'am? Are you in danger?"

"Mmmmhmph...:"

"Ma'am, is someone there with you?"

"Oh... god..."

"Ma'am...? Are you alo-... Can you get somewhere safe?"

"Stay on the line with me and hide, ok? Stay on the line so I can direct the police to you. OK, ma'am?"

'Unit 517, there's a possible 240 in progress at 579 Sycamore Lane. Bus dispatched. Proceed with caution, that's a 10-31.'

"Ma'am?"

'*Sto...*'

"Ma'am, the police are on their way, ok? Just stay hidden and keep me on the line."

"Ma'am, are you there?"

"Ma'am?"

EN MEDIAS RES

I SEE them jump as if I was watching a movie. They cut the air, hair flying, eyes trained on the spot they would inevitably land. As they descend, something snaps inside me and tells me I'd better get going. No sense making it easy for them.

I crouch and run, digging in, hauling ass.

I hear them behind me, the sound of their grunts and growls ringing in my ear.

I could feel the heat of their breath on my neck.

I broke the door—damn it, I broke it and it can't help me now, can't slow them down, can't create a barrier between us. Thinking about the destruction my ill-placed hit caused slows my feet and the one called Hawkish is upon me, tackling me to the floor in the middle of the orange room: an oasis amidst the chaos. The orange room. This is where they bring the happy people, the ones who get to leave after a short visit and smell the flowers, feel the air on their skin. This is where I will breathe my last breath.

I turn to face my captor; my killer. He hoists me up; slams me against the wall; throws me around like a rag doll, but it doesn't matter. Hawkish hurts me. He always has.

He's saying something threatening as per usual, challenging my audacity to attack the one who somehow makes being a halfling sound like committing a sin, leaning close to intimidate me into acquiescence, but it doesn't matter. Not this time. I can't help the faint smile that plays at the corner of my lips at the sight of the blood that trickled from his hairline.

I can hurt too.

A CHRISTMAS TALE

SHE COULD FEEL it before she opened the door; something dropped in her stomach as she reached for the doorknob, protesting, begging her to turn away... to leave. *I hate that tree*, Marley thought as soon as she walked into her house, the blinking lights accosting her before she could close the door. Green. Red. Orange. Blue. White. Blinking fast then slow, then fast again because her mother hadn't set the speed, just left the lights to cycle through whatever the factory setting was. Marley knew they were Christmas lights, but they felt like eyes when she came in the room and saw them there, changing color while she watched...

...almost like they were winking at her.

Winking at her from behind gaudy Christmas ornaments clustered in front; ornaments that almost drowned out the incessant blinking.

Almost.

Marley groaned as she walked in, unable to pull her eyes away from the monstrosity.

The *monster*.

She eyed it and from somewhere beneath the lights and ornaments, and tinsel, it stared back at her.

Marley walked toward the tree, walking deeper into the living room scattered with the storage bins that held those offensive ornaments and other collected tree trash for most of the year, her shoulders instinctively raising higher and higher with every step. She didn't feel it happening but knew what was going on. Marley was preparing herself to fight, preparing herself for battle.

Because it was in there. And this year she was going to get it out.

The wind whipped outside the open front door, pushing in the cold air and letting out the warm, but Marley didn't feel the chill on the air. She threw her backpack to the floor; she needed her hands free for what was to come.

Marley's chest heaved as the tree vibrated and thrummed.

The tree reached out to Marley, surprising her.. She craned her neck, cringing, spine arching, desperate not to feel the coarse bristles against her skin as the branches elongated, stretched their plastic tips toward Marley's face. Her feet tangled beneath her and she shrieked in surprise as she fell, a sound she wished she hadn't made because now her mother would come to see what was wrong; her mother would come and ask why the door was open... her mother would see what lived in the tree and it would go after her too.

Its bloody mouth spread into a smile as if it could read Marley's thoughts.

Marley could see its eyes now, set deep in the thick of the fake tree that was older than she was. Marley knew her mother had played Christmas songs by Johnny Mathis and drank wine as she trimmed the tree just like she did every year, and just like every year before that one, the beast in the tree woke up, blinked its hateful eyes, and waited. For what,

Marley didn't know. Maybe for Marley to get too close so it could stick its metal fasteners in one of her eyes or scratch her face as she reached for presents?

Her mother never seemed to notice.

Maybe, Marley had time to wonder, *it was just waiting for* me.

Marley's hair pulled from her scalp as a branch she hadn't noticed wound itself around a few braids... enough to hurt... enough to trap her. Marley wanted to scream, wanted to call for help, but the branches pressed into her mouth, ripping her tongue from her jaw and diving through the tunnel of her throat to strangle her breath.

Some of the tinsel on the lower branches was knocked loose and tangled itself in Marley's hair as she was dragged under it... into it; it was the perfect wrapping for the perfect gift. Joanne came up from the basement with another bin full of ornaments and put them on the floor in front of the tree. She stood straight and placed her hands on her hips, tired from walking up the stairs mostly but also because there really wasn't any more room for more ornaments.

She plumped the limbs, marveling at how such an old tree could still look brand new, full and flush like she felt after a satisfying meal. Then she spotted it.

Maybe there is *room for a few more*, Joanne thought as she smiled, *right there, where Marley dropped her bag.*

THE COLOR OF BLOOD

"WHAT DO you make of it, Detective?" he finally asked after staring at the side of Richardson's face long enough to be uncomfortable. He knew the question was coming but didn't have an answer; the officer, fresh on the street by the looks of it, could have watched him for hours and Richardson still wouldn't have known what to say.

"Hard to tell," he started and let his words linger, deciding that was enough. He had poked the bloody shirt with the end of his pen and knelt next to the conspicuous dark spot on the porch long enough to have more than that, but nothing was coming to him, none of the ideas he was known for around the office. The detective he shadowed during his first few months in plain clothes used to say it was like he had committed the murders himself, gave him the side eye every once in a while like he really believed it might be true. Back in the precinct they settled on him having second sight, being clairvoyant, seeing things; the words changed depending upon who was saying them, but not the sentiment. He told them they'd better be careful talking like that; the brass might take their badges and require psych eval before they could get them back. They'd laugh and so would he, but they still wondered how Richardson was able to figure out the most obscure cases —the woman whose skin looked like she had been in the water for days but had just been pronounced dead 30 minutes before; the mummified digit lying in the middle of a busy street. He always figured it out—that's probably why they'd called him for this one. He wasn't up next. Hell, he had been thinking about taking a few days off in Syosset.

Richardson looked over at the front door of the place. It was weathered and old, warped from years of swelling in the sun and settling against bitter winter winds. It needed a coat of paint and so did the porch he was standing on, both more like the weathered wood of an old barn than the cookie-cutter facades of suburbia. Curious. More than that. Downright odd. Because there was an HOA in place and homeowner's associations didn't take too kindly to people not keeping up their homes. Property value was a thing, and it seemed the HOA's sole purpose was to complain about lawns not being trimmed or flowerbeds in disarray. If painting the shutters bright pink could get an owner fined, leaving the front to wither in the elements had to be cause for concern. Richardson looked on his phone to make sure he'd gotten it right. It felt funny doing it even though it's all he'd ever known. When he was growing up and the people around him called him by his first name rather than his last, he watched all the police shows on TV. Columbo, Kojak, Magnum P.I., T.J. Hooker. He wanted to be like all of them. And he was, at least an amalgamation of them, though he doubted any of them would have appreciated the device he spoke into in his hand to take notes... except maybe Inspector Gadget.

It was the second note he had taken and yep, he'd heard the beat cop correctly: Someone at the HOA called the police after walking around the grounds and smelling something foul.

Richardson smelled it too, and it was strong.

What the busybody from the HOA didn't know—what the stench didn't allow him to trespass further to figure out—was that all the windows were closed too so the source of the smell must be fresh and there was likely more than one. That bothered Richardson, of course, but what made his hair stand on end was how they had gotten to that state, the two people inside whose blood had seeped into the floorboards of different rooms, rooms that had seen gatherings and celebrations and happy times before their deaths. Because the door had been nailed shut from the inside.

The door to the front, the doors to the bedroom where the father lay dead. The note they found made it sound like she had killed him, slit his throat because she was angry, she was tired, she was finished. Her friends said they didn't see it coming, said they had been out that night and she was happy, so happy, too happy to have done this... killed him and then herself... and then her son? What about her son? Where was he when this happened? Why was his door free of nails? Had he not tried to protect himself from his mother? Had she gotten him as he fled? The bloody shirt Richardson kept worrying with his pen said maybe. But then where was his body?

Nailed shut. Nailed inside. If slit from ear to ear, he wouldn't have had the strength to try to keep her out that way, find boards and nails and a hammer and bang. He would lose too much blood if the energy was exerted like that; there would be a pool of it by the door. But there wasn't. Indeed, there wasn't a drop spilled.

And the mother... would she have gouged out her eyes the way she had if she had done what the letter said she did? She meant to do it, it said. She knew what she was doing and she meant it all. But Oedipus gouged his eyes out because he couldn't bear to see his life laid bare the way it was anymore. Had she? She bled through the sockets, bled through the holes she made in her head, bled until she had nothing left. Her last few words damned her, condemned her, sent her straight to hell for spilling her child and husband's blood, and then she bled on the floor where she sat. On the floor across from her son's room.

Richardson poked at the shirt again then called someone over to tag it. Generic brand cotton pullover—nothing that couldn't be bought at any store anywhere. It would be tested, analyzed, the blood staining it compared to the parents and it would be a DNA match—Richardson knew that. But none of that would tell him what he needed to know.

Where was he?

Neighbors said they hadn't seen him in a while, that they hadn't seen the parents either, but that was no big surprise. Work, school, the things that keep the wheels turning—those are the things that force people into their houses in the evening, deposit them on the sofa until 2 a.m. when they wake up to find the TV watching them. Nobody saw anything. Nobody ever did.

The shirt didn't have to be his, Richardson tried to tell himself but he knew better. The shirt didn't have to be his— it could be someone else's, a bum off the street who decided to roam the suburban neighborhood he found himself in and ditch what was likely one of his only garments because it had a little blood on it, all this in the chill of early spring. And the mother didn't have to be covering for someone—her words, the ones she had written with such a heavy hand that she broke through the paper in a few places before scrawling her name, they could have been the god's honest truth when they said she hated her family and hated herself and wanted them all to die. Her, she had said emphatically—she was the one who hated them all and had done this. The father had tried to say something, more of the same Richardson thought, but they would never know. His writing was unfinished, 'It's m —' as far as he got, the letters jagged and oddly spaced, written in blood. Everything could be as it looked. It wouldn't take much to connect dots that shouldn't be connected, make up a story that was just plausible enough to be believed. If he went to one of the cops standing around looking at him, busying themselves, waiting for a cue from him about what to do next—if he went to one of them and said that one or the other of them did it, mounted a decent enough argument for why he thought so, they would call it a murder suicide and it would be over. The DNA match on the shirt wouldn't point a finger at the son—it would just prove that the blood on the shirt was a match for the dead people in the house. And of course it was—one of them used it, after all.

Easy paperwork.

Wrapped up crime scene.

Pat... because no one could nail up a door behind them, not from the inside.

Murder suicide, sure. That's what it looked like and that's what it would be. Except the woman in the window looking toward the sun and crying black tears told him otherwise.

STRANGERS: A REIMAGINING

THE WAITRESS WATCHED them from behind the beaded curtain, the American and his lady. They were upset with each other, but trying to look serene, as if any drunk stumbling out of the bar couldn't see what was going on. They looked out at the hills, gazing off in the distance at some unknown thing, hoping to defer their problem, to give it over to the hills as a form of offering. But it didn't work. It never works, no matter how many people stand in that very spot trying to do the very same thing.

The heat was oppressive inside the kitchen where the waitress stood, one ear to the conversation in front of her and one listening to the cook who was humming while he chopped, but it didn't deter her. She could have ducked into the walk-in and felt the cool air on her skin—only a second would have been needed in respite—but she didn't want to miss anything. He was trying to convince the lady to do something, something she didn't really want to do. He didn't want to make it seem like he was, but there was desperation on his face. The waitress felt sorry for the woman; she looked like she was losing her very soul as the conversation trod on. She thought maybe she would interrupt them, offer more water, tell them of the man that lives on the other side of the very hills they stared at, and his reclusive ways—something to break the flow. Maybe that would help the woman regain some of herself. Maybe she would find a way to hold her chin up and finish the conversation with dignity.

The waitress looked at the clock. The train would be there in 5 minutes. This was her chance.

The waitress put down the beer and ceremoniously announced the coming of the train, just as the lady threatened to scream. The American gathered himself and left the table, looking as appreciative for the separation as she hoped the woman felt. With a demure smile playing at the corners of her lips, the waitress faded into the recesses of the kitchen, saying a silent prayer for the woman, so tortured yet so graceful, sitting on the platform alone.[1]

---

1. Editor's Note: This story reimagines the action and setting of Ernest Hemingway's classic short story, "Hills Like White Elephants," first published in the August 1927 issue of the literary magazine *transition*, then later that year in Hemingway's short story collection, *Men Without Women*. This author has given Hemingway's "girl" a much more empathetic witness.

THE CALL

THE BLOOD always calls to me.

I always hear it beg for release, a gift I cannot give... I *should* not give. It beckons me do its bidding in the evening, caressing the words, teasing my earlobe with its feathered touch. The darkness masks its face, leaving me defenseless and blind as I reach for it to sate and be sated. Ay, but no, I shall not give in this time. I will not let it manipulate me for its wanton desires. The blood must be controlled even as it threatens to deny my very existence.

I lay covering my ears, denying purchase, but it finds other ways to make me weak. I bend to its will even when I resist. My body does not agree with my mind and falls prey all too easily, each and every time.

On the edge of the bed I sit awaiting the next touch, the next whisper; the next command. I look out of the window at the vast city below, its people sleeping their mindless sleep, reveling in the façade that is serenity, and laugh despite myself.

DENIAL

"BECAUSE I DON'T WANT TO!"

That's the last thing he said before he turned off like a light switch. He was there, still there... awake, if not fully aware. I knew because I could hear him. I knew because there was no reason for him not to be—25-year-old man in good health and fine spirits before he went inside. I knew because he had to be... if he wasn't, the world didn't make sense, would never make sense again.

"Babe, come out," I whispered, even though I heard the world crack open and swallow him whole, body and soul.

ANYMORE

His hands were on her and then they weren't.

He was pawing, prying, panting in anticipation, pressing down on her so she couldn't get up, couldn't move, couldn't breathe...

... but then he wasn't.

He wasn't because he wasn't anymore.

He wasn't hot anymore, not game anymore, not *him* anymore.

He wasn't... anything, not anymore.

He said nobody would notice.

He said even if they did, nobody would stop him because they would be too busy saving their own asses to care what he was doing out there, right out in the open.

Because it was all over.

He laughed at her.

Called her stupid.

Because she didn't see it, didn't believe it would happen, didn't think the world would be wiped away.

As he lay on top of her, tears springing from his eyes like fire hydrant flow interrupted by a big stick, drenching his face as he pulled at himself, tugged at it, flaccid thing that it was, terrified into permanent inaction, but still he pulled and pulled and pulled. With the other hand he squeezed her breast, twisted it like the crank of a Jack-in-the-Box, fingers bruising, digging into her flesh. He heard her squealing, but no, he didn't care because it was over, it was over, it was fucking over, goddamn it, couldn't she see that? Who gave a shit anymore?

When his head split in half, a diagonal slice that looked like it was made with a sword, she didn't cry for him. The squealing that had been issuing forth from her mouth minutes before died in her throat as the sky behind him first went black then blossomed with the most brilliant of reds like Heaven was on fire. She choked on her screams as she heard people dropping around her, falling to the ground dead, dead, so very dead. She could see inside some of them, holes bored through their foreheads to show their brains, through their chests, all the way out of their backs.

Carol from the diner. She must have left food in the window to run out of the place before the lasers came to kill all of them, cold and impersonal like sunlight through a magnifying glass over an ant colony. The beam cut into her body, opening her with the precision of a surgeon. Carol fell right behind where she and Buster, the bastard who died with his limp dick in his hands, lay in the street. Carol fell on her back, her stomach open where she'd been sliced, intestines spilling out like they were too big for the cavity they had been crammed into.

Walker and his wife. Was her name Maggie? Margaret? Misty? Marla? She didn't remember, and it didn't matter, not anymore. They fell next to where she lay under that bastard, Buster, close enough that Walker's arm flung onto her shoulder when he landed, their eyes burned out, burned clear through their heads.

She could hear the hiss of the beams coming from some unseen thing in the sky. Must be a UFO, she thought, but even then, she wasn't so sure. It was just something she would have said twenty minutes before, when all she had to worry about was what she was going to have for dinner.

Aliens.

That's what people thought of when terror came from the sky, right? That's what they said in the movies, like aliens didn't have anything else to do but to mess with the good people of Earth and take over the planet like squatters.

Buster smelled of cheap cologne and his own piss and shit.

She looked left, saw the kid whose only job was to gather up the carts from the parking lot and bring them inside. He couldn't have been more than 16 years old, probably went to the high school down the street from where they both lay. The carts were on top of him—the little ones meant for just a few items; the big ones for Thanksgiving dinner-type shopping. There was even a cart designed for kids to pretend they were driving sitting on top of him, the handle attached to a racecar cockpit with a steering wheel and everything. This one had landed on his head after the wind that came behind the lasers swept through, wind strong enough to push carts full of food abandoned by their owners across the lot...well, at least partially: some carts still had limbs attached to them, fingers gripping tight in death even as the arms they belonged to were severed at the elbows. The wind was strong enough to uproot street signs and carry them over the highway and up the hill to where she was pinned beneath Buster. Decatur Street. That was at least a mile away, she thought. She wondered what was happening on Decatur Street then, whether or not someone was surveying the aftermath like she was from a similar perch, stuck beneath the rubble and rot.

She looked right and saw more of the same. Downed bodies covered in blood, organs on the ground covered in the dirt that had been pulled loose in the windstorm, innards dredged in viscous fluid and coated in soil like a snack ready to be pan fried and served up to who? The aliens? The gods?

Something stringy and wet flapped toward her propelled by the wind but tethered to something on one side. She recoiled beneath Buster, disgusted because she thought that the pink, fleshy thing was sinew even though she had never seen a picture of sinew to know for sure. She wriggled, desperate to get away from it, single-minded in that effort now that she had convinced herself about what it was. It kept flapping toward her, reaching for her. She was sure that if it touched her, it would consume her, eat away at her like acid, skin ulcering like a canker sore on the sensitive pink of one's lip, falling off in big clumps... flesh-eating disease in the end because why not? She laughed, the prospect enough to break her resolve, to tip her over the edge and send her into hysterics.

And nobody cared.

A thought came to mind as her laughter trailed off, an elaborate picture show forming in her head to display everything in graphic detail.

Maybe the stuff she thought was sinew was really a spore like in that old alien invasion movie. Maybe if it touched her, she'd see it turn *into* her, first morphing from the stringy crap into a blob, then forming a face that looked like hers, a body that was tall and slender, gangly when pressed into action, like her own. Maybe it would open its eyes and stare at her, shoot a fleshy appendage out to touch her face, feel the contours so the replica would be better... more authentic. Then she laughed again, the sound harsh in the deafening quiet. She laughed in part because of the beast made of sinew, the monster after her essence, but mostly because she realized she was going to die beneath that bastard, Buster, after all. She was going die after surviving the fucking apocalypse, managing to dodge hot globs of flying flesh and lasers intent on cutting everyone in half. She was going to die because she couldn't breathe underneath his body anymore, his dead weight feeling like a ton of bricks on top of her thin body. She was going to die because she was afraid to get out from under him, afraid to stand exposed in the crowded parking lot where she'd be utterly alone. The laser would find her if she did.

When the librarian had fallen, she had lost her shoe.

The old guy who picked up trash off the street in town had lost his teeth when his head hit the ground unprotected, unshielded, smacking against the asphalt hard enough to break the thin skin over his skull and spew blood. She had to crane her neck to see him, could have avoided that particular sight, but she couldn't stop herself from moving, from stretching, from trying to see. His mouth was open, jaw permanently set in a surprised 'O'.

It was quiet. Quiet, but not silent.

Fuzzy.

The way one might think static would sound.

She listened to it. Closed her eyes and tried to fall asleep to it. Maybe when she woke up she'd be ready to move, ready to make a run for it, just in case the laser was waiting for her.

Maybe when she woke up, she'd be dead.

She squeezed her eyes shut.

Buster's blood dripped onto her face, into her mouth.

The sinew monster took another swipe at her, getting closer this time.

She shrieked at the thought of it making contact, attaching itself to her skin, sucking at her with toothy mouths that dotted its flesh. She found strength she didn't know she had, pushed Buster's mutilated body over to the side, and stood up on shaky legs.

She was out.

She was out.

She turned around in a circle, surveying the lot.

She was alone.

Bodies strewn around, torsos here, limbs there. Scalps, fingers, livers, hearts—she thought of Humpty Dumpty when he fell off the wall, a grisly puzzle with the pieces lying on a table, some right side up, some upside down. She grabbed at her arms, reached for her legs, looked at her shoes, still on her feet, and wriggled her toes, checking even though she could feel herself, knew everything was still where it should be, but because nobody else around her was intact, she looked at herself anyway, to be sure. Then she looked back at Buster. That asshole, Buster, who always looked at her with kind eyes when he said hello; Buster, who always seemed to be coming when she was going, always happened to be wherever she was; Buster, who she thought was harmless right up until he threw her to the ground to have his way because the world was ending.

Buster, who had saved her life by getting on top of her.

She saw the bodies around them and realized something that made her angry.

He had been right.

Nobody cared.

Carol, the librarian, the garbage picker, Walker and whatever his wife's name was, all the people who had met the laser close by her and Buster, so close they could have touched them, screamed at him, pushed him off of her—none of them cared about what Buster was doing. They were too busy trying the save their own asses to worry about anything else.

But the laser saw.

The laser knew all.

The kid with the carts was looking at her with a smile on his face as a bubble of bloody spit grew large on the corner of his mouth, like gum.

And that didn't matter either.

Because he wasn't anything anymore.